WINNING BID

Marge O'Day had come to Skye Fargo's room for one overriding reason. She wanted the Trailsman to take her stagecoach over a trail of terror to a destination it seemed dead sure not to reach.

"Money didn't do it with you," she told Skye. "I though maybe something else might."

"I'm listening," Fargo said.

Marge turned to fully face him and her hand began to undo a row of buttons that went down the front of her dress. When she reached those at her waist, the top of the dress fell open, slipped from her shoulders and cascaded to the floor. Marge stood there, totally naked and still as a statue, letting Fargo's eyes feast their full.

Skye Fargo's gun was for hire—and this fee looked tempting as hell. . . .

THE TRAILSMAN 63

STAGECOACH TO HELL

by

Jon Sharpe

A SIGNET BOOK

NEW AMERICAN LIBRARY

PUBLISHER'S NOTE

This novel is a work of fiction. Names, characters, places, and incidents either are the product of the author's imagination or are used fictitiously, and any resemblance to actual persons, living or dead, events, or locales is entirely coincidental.

All rights reserved
The first chapter of this book
appeared in *Horsethief Crossing*,
the sixty-second book in this series.

SIGNET TRADEMARK REG. U.S. PAT. OFF. AND FOREIGN COUNTRIES
REGISTERED TRADEMARK—MARCA REGISTRADA
HECHO EN CHICAGO, U.S.A.

SIGNET, SIGNET CLASSIC, MENTOR, ONYX, PLUME, MERIDIAN
AND NAL BOOKS are published by New American Library,
1633 Broadway, New York, New York 10019

First Printing, March, 1987

1 2 3 4 5 6 7 8 9

PRINTED IN THE UNITED STATES OF AMERICA

The Trailsman

Beginnings . . . they bend the tree and they mark the man. Skye Fargo was born when he was eighteen. Terror was his midwife, vengeance his first cry. Killing spawned Skye Fargo, ruthless, cold-blooded murder. Out of the acrid smoke of gunpowder still hanging in the air, he rose, cried out a promise never forgotten.

The Trailsman, they began to call him, all across the West: searcher, scout, hunter, the man who could see where others only looked, his skills for hire but not his soul, the man who lived each day to the fullest, yet trailed each tomorrow. Skye Fargo, the Trailsman, the seeker who could take the wildness of a land and the wanting of a woman and make them his own.

1860, the Montana–Idaho border.

The White man gave the land names;
Lost Trail Pass, Trapper Peak, Pioneer Mountain.
The Crow simply called the land . . . "ours."

1

He hadn't expected company.

And he certainly hadn't expected to be shot at naked in a pond.

But that was exactly what was happening as two more bullets grazed his ear. Fargo dived underwater as he flung another glance at the two horsemen at the edge of the small, spring-fed pond. They both fired again, the shots muffled sounds underwater as the Trailsman swam deeper. He leveled off, struck out and surfaced at the opposite edge. He shook water from his eyes and saw the two horsemen start to race around the pond toward him. He swore softly. His clothes and gun were where he had neatly placed them on the far bank. The two riders would be at him in moments and he lifted himself, dived underwater again, glimpsing the tiny spirals of spray where two bullets slammed into the water only inches from him.

He stayed underwater until he ran out of air and surfaced in the center of the pond. The two men had halted at opposite sides of the small pond and a pair of shots bracketed him instantly. He sank again as he cursed inwardly. He couldn't keep surfacing without his luck running out, he realized as he made a half-circle underwater. They wanted him dead. He'd have to let them think they got what they wanted and he struck out hard. He surfaced at full stroke, arms and legs flailing, as he appeared to be trying to reach the far edge of the pond. He sent up sprays and splashes of water as he swam with more haste and fury than skill and the flurry of shots sounded at once. He heard three bullets slap the water as he swam and he let out a yell of pain, throwing one arm up in the air. He filled his lungs with air as he flipped over in the water and sank.

"We got him," he heard one of the men shout. Fargo stayed down as long as he could and when his chest grew tight and he felt the sharp, burning pain of lungs about to explode, he let himself go to the surface. He kept his naked body facedown as he surfaced but managed to draw in a gasp of air out of one corner of his mouth. He lay floating inertly, legs still, face submerged, a naked, floating corpse. "I told you we got him," he heard the rider shout.

Fargo stayed motionless in the water and heard one of the horses start to trot, rein up, halt for a moment, then go on. He listened, let the sound of both horses grow dim as the two riders cantered away. He lifted his head enough to draw in another mouthful of air and turned onto his side only when the sound of hoofbeats died away completely. "Bastards," he swore as he swam to the edge of the pond where he'd left his clothes. He swore again as he saw that they'd taken his gun and the calf holster with the slender double-edged throwing knife inside it. He walked to the Ovaro where the horse rested a few yards from the pond, took a towel from his saddlebag and dried off before pulling on clothes. He swung onto the Ovaro, his eyes on the tracks left by the two horsemen. They had gone north and he followed, a furrow clinging to his brow.

It had all happened so quickly, so completely unexpectedly and with no reason. But there was a reason, he knew. There was always a reason, even for the seemingly senseless. He had come upon the little spring-fed pond nestled in the hills and it had seemed the perfect spot for a cool and cleansing dip after two days of trail riding. He'd waited, scanned the surrounding terrain for signs of Crow or perhaps passing Nez Percé or Mandan. But mostly he watched for Crow. They had been growing increasingly less tolerant of intruders on the land they looked upon as theirs. But there'd been nothing but a pair of mule deer and a pronghorn and he'd happily shed clothes and plunged into the cold, clear water.

He'd only been in the pond for a few minutes when the two horsemen had appeared, riding full out. They came charging out of the hawthorns at the east side of the pond, saw him in the water as he saw them, a case of mutual surprise. But they had instantly unholstered six-guns and began throwing lead at him. He had dived, his only recourse to prevent being shot full of holes. Fargo felt the furrow dig deeper into his brow as he followed the hoofprints. The two men had reacted at once when they saw him looking at them. Whatever their reasons, it was all-important to them that he not be around to tell anyone he'd seen them. Were they running to something or from something? His mouth tightened into a thin line. What mattered more was that they were so ready and willing to kill him just for seeing them. Anger at the thought spiraled inside him as he followed the tracks down into a narrow dip of land.

He saw both horses shorten fore and rear hoofprints. They had slowed as they entered a woodland of white fir and Fargo took the Ovaro into the woods, stayed on the trail of hoofprints and reined to a halt when he heard voices. He swung silently from the saddle and moved forward on foot, finally left the Ovaro with the reins dropped across a long branch and crept on alone. The two men came into sight, halted beside a stream. Both were out of the saddle, kneeling alongside the stream as they refilled canteens and the horses drank. Fargo took in the two figures, both ordinary, nondescript types, both medium height, one with the trace of a blond mustache, the other with dark stubble along his chin. Fargo saw his Colt, gunbelt and calf holster hanging from the saddlehorn of one horse and returned his eyes to the two men.

He swore silently. There was no way he could reach them without being shot full of lead by one or the other. His eyes narrowed as he glanced back along the trail through the firs. The two men had set a fairly straight line and he decided to bank on their continuing on straight when they crossed the stream. He pushed himself to his feet and retreated a half dozen yards, moved on steps silent as a cougar's pads. He made a wide circle, leaped across the stream when he came to it again and doubled back down along the far side. The two men were still resting their horses, their voices muffled through the woods. Fargo halted beside a full, thick-limbed fir and began to pull himself up into the tree. He halted astride a low branch that bore enough foliage to conceal and enough knobby places to grip.

Fargo stretched his long legs out along the branch and waited. He had to take out one man with a single, quick, ruthless move and make the other one come to him. They hadn't thought twice about trying to kill him in the pond. He'd return the favor, Fargo commented silently, his lake-blue eyes cold as ice floes. He pushed aside idle thoughts as his wild-creature hearing picked up the sounds of a horse stepping into the stream to cross to the other bank. The two riders came into view a few minutes after and Fargo's eyes followed the two men as they approached through the woods below. The one with the dark stubble rode closest to the tree, Fargo noted, his horse a few steps behind the other. They were almost passing beneath him, and Fargo drew his legs forward on the branch, tensed powerful shoulder muscles and steel-spring thighs. He watched the two men come almost under the tree, counted off ten seconds more and lifted himself up on the branch. He sprang as the mountain lion springs, a long, sweeping arc, every muscle taut, every fiber of his being aimed at the target, a missile of concentrated power.

Fargo slammed into the nearest rider with awesome fury, wrapped one arm around the man's neck as he swept the figure off the horse. He twisted as he fell, landed half atop the man and he heard the sharp cracking sound of neck vertebrae snapping. He released his grip on the already limp figure and rolled sideways into a clump of bittersweet, stayed low and saw the second man wheeling his horse around, six-gun in hand. But the rider was still recovering from his surprise, his gun raised but not aimed. Fargo rolled again inside the bittersweet, the sound drawing two shots at once, both too fast and too high. He let himself roll again, came up against the base of a big fir. A third shot slammed into the tree with a shower of wood chips.

Fargo twisted his big frame to scurry around to the other side of the tree and the man fired again. The Trailsman's lips edged a grim smile. The man continued to shoot too quickly from a poor angle. Fargo drew up on one knee on the other side of the tree, glanced to his rear and spotted the line of thick sweetfern. He waited, heard the rider send his horse charging forward. When he saw the horse's snout come into sight he flung himself backward into the sweetfern, stayed low in the thick brush as the shot whistled over his head. He pushed forward, peered back through the brush and saw the man racing toward him, his face an angry half-snarl. He pulled his horse up sharply as Fargo rolled to his left, then back to his right, fired again and the shot was wide of its mark.

"Six," Fargo spit out as he leapt to his feet and charged out of the brush into the open. The man fired again and cursed as he heard only the click of an empty chamber.

"Bastard," the rider snarled and spurred his horse forward at the big man that charged toward him. Fargo let the horse race at him, swerved with only an inch of space left and felt the powerful shoulders and forequarters brush past him. But he was reaching up, closed his arms around the man's leg as the horse raced by. With a curse and a shout, the rider came out of the saddle, Fargo hanging on to his leg with both arms. The man hit the ground on his back, Fargo falling with him to land half across his chest. He twisted away as the man swung the empty six-gun in a short arc, rolled aside and leaped to his feet. He came in, avoided a second swing of the gun barrel as the man used the gun as a short club. Fargo lashed out with a left, purposely short, and the man came in over it with the gun raised, brought the weapon down in a short, chopping motion. Fargo pulled away from the blow, crossed a looping right that caught the man high on the cheekbone with enough force to make him stagger back. Fargo's long-armed left shot out, cracked against the man's jaw and the figure went backward, stumbled, fell to one knee.

Fargo stepped forward, lashed out with a long, low, sweeping left hook, but the man surprised him. He came in instead of trying to pull back, wrapped both arms around Fargo's legs and yanked. Fargo felt himself go down hard on his back, the man's arms still gripping his legs. He yanked back on his right leg and the man let go, tried to dive forward on top of him. Fargo brought his leg up and

15

his knee caught the man in the chest and the figure fell to one side. Fargo started to push to his feet but the man flung himself sideways, crashed into him at the ankles, and Fargo felt his feet go out from under him.

He pitched forward, tried to twist his body to the side and failed. His right knee came down with all his weight behind it full on the man's throat and he heard the gasped, gurgled sound that erupted along with a small gusher of red. Fargo let himself go forward, across the man's body, rolled to his feet and watched the figure twitch convulsively as the stream of red grew stronger. He grimaced, cursing silently. Neither of the two would be answering any questions. When the figure gave a last, shuddered twitch and lay still, Fargo stepped around it to the horse, retrieved his gunbelt and Colt and the calf holster and knife. He walked slowly back through the woods, crossed the small stream to where he'd left the Ovaro and climbed into the saddle.

He retraced his steps back to the pond, not hurrying, a frown creasing his brow. Curiosity more than anything else made him continue east as he picked up the trail where the two riders had come upon him in the pond. They'd been riding hard all the way, he saw from the prints that dug deeply into the ground, and he followed the clear, fresh trail down a long slope of wooded terrain. As the ground leveled off and the woods thinned out, he saw a road appear ahead, a bend almost directly in front of him. He reached it and halted, his eyes scanning the ground. The two riders had left the road at the bend and struck out north, where they'd eventually come upon him in the pond.

The bend turned out to be a long, slow curve and it wasn't till he reached the other end of it that he saw the stagecoach halted in the middle of the road. A small knot of figures clustered around the outside of the coach and as he rode closer he saw that the two lead horses of what had been a four-horse team were missing. The front ends of the harness shafts were dipped low and two sets of breast collars, bellybands and check reins lay on the ground. Fargo saw a man step forward and wave at him as he drew up to the stage and he let his glance sweep all the figures standing by. He saw two men, three women, an old lady and a little boy he guessed to be about seven years old.

"We're sure glad to see you, mister," the man said in a smooth voice and Fargo took in a gray suit, a gray Stetson and a light blue four-in-hand with a pearl stickpin. The man had a clean-shaven face made round by food, not by structure. "We've got troubles." The man nodded toward the stage. Fargo saw with one quick glance that it was no heavy Concord but a Brewster converted roadcoach, the driver's seat detached from the main body of the passenger compartment, and an extra rear seat built high at the rear. Not so durable or heavy as the rugged Concords used by most stage lines across the west, the Brewster roadcoach had a touch more elegance of line, could hold more passengers and take a smaller team. "I'm Cyrus Holman," the man said and Fargo nodded as his eyes went to the others.

"Marge O'Day," a woman said and stepped forward and Fargo took in a woman about thirty to thirty-five, big bust under a gray cotton dress, a little on the heavy side all over, a broad face under thick, curly blond hair that had been tinkered with to make it blonder, a face that had seen everything and could still laugh. A man with a woman clinging to his arm moved away from alongside the coach, gray-haired, well-dressed, a tension in his face that made him seem more than the sixty-odd years he carried. The woman was half his age, Fargo saw, attractive with a thin, long nose, dark-brown hair pulled back in a knot and dark-blue eyes that mocked the way she clung to his arm.

"Delwin Ferris," the man said with a trace of authoritativeness. "My secretary and traveling companion, Myrna Sayres." The woman returned Fargo's nod with a smile of cool interest. "We'd be most obliged for any help you can give us, mister." Ferris managed to make the statement sound like an order.

Fargo's glance moved to the little old lady and he saw a small frame, not much over five-feet two inches, snapping blue eyes under a bright blue bonnet, steel-gray hair and a thin, sharp face. "Pauline Beal, young feller," she said in a voice that matched the snapping blue eyes. Fargo kept the smile inside himself as he turned his gaze on the young woman and the boy. He saw dark blond hair that hung loosely down to her shoulders, a very pretty, fine-featured face with high cheekbones and lips that would be soft and full but for the tight way she held her mouth. But it was her eyes that held him, early-morning eyes, a dusky, cloudy blue.

"I'm Charity Foster," she said as he took in a slender figure with modest full breasts under a square-necked dress. "This is Mitchell Blake," she said, introducing the little boy. "I'm Mitchell's governess." Fargo allowed a nod as he swung from the Ovaro and stepped to the stagecoach with Cyrus Holman beside him.

"Looks as though you lost half your team," Fargo commented.

"Lost isn't the word." Cyrus Holman bristled. "They were taken, stolen, made off with right out of the harness."

Fargo's eyes narrowed. "Two men?" he asked.

"Why, yes." Holman frowned. "You see them?"

"I think so," Fargo answered. "Let me guess. They hailed you and you stopped and they took two of your horses at gunpoint, right?"

"Not exactly," Holman said. "They didn't hail us. They were our driver and shotgun rider. They just pulled to a halt, made everybody get out and held a gun to us while they unhitched the horses. Then they rode off and left us here."

"Just like that? No talk? No robbing you? Nothing else?" Fargo frowned.

"Not a damn thing. They just took the horses and hightailed it," the man said.

Fargo's frown stayed as thoughts tumbled through his mind. "Something's wrong. Something doesn't smell right," he muttered.

"Meaning what?" Holman asked.

"I saw your two men. They tried to kill me for it," Fargo said. "That doesn't add up. They stole two horses and abandoned you. That's not enough reason for all the trouble they went to to try and kill me for seeing them. What else were they running from?"

"Search me," Holman said. "All I know is what they did to us."

"Not enough. They were riding too hard, killing too quick. Something stinks," Fargo growled. He slowly scanned the others as they watched him, saw apprehension, uncertainty and tightness in their faces. All except Pauline Beal. In the little old lady's face he saw only irritation and impatience. His gaze lifted, moved beyond the knot of figures and the stagecoach. He'd caught the movement in the trees lining the slope, watched and saw the leaves move again in a steady procession that meant only one thing. He kept his eyes at the top of the slope as the others followed his gaze and he heard their quick gasps as the shapes moved out of the foilage. Three riders, first, then three more followed by another cluster and still another until Fargo counted fourteen near-naked bronzed bodies glistening in the sun.

Delwin Ferris broke the silence. "By God, there's the answer. Those two rotten cowards must have spotted the Crow and decided to run for it and save their own necks at our expense."

"Yes, that's it," Cyrus Holman agreed.

Fargo, his eyes on the slope, heard Marge O'Day's voice cut in, a trace of grim amusement in it. "The big man doesn't agree," she said.

Fargo turned to her and allowed a slow smile. "Give the lady a cigar," he said. "And the name's Fargo, Skye Fargo."

"Of course that's the explanation," Delwin Ferris insisted.

"If they were just running to save their necks why'd they take so much time trying to kill me?" Fargo said. "There's no law against being a coward and a bastard. Something still stinks." His eyes went back to the slope and he heard the bitter edge in his voice. "But it looks as though I'm not going to be finding out what," he muttered as he peered up at the bronzed riders.

2

"What are they waiting for? We're defenseless," Myrna Sayres said, panic in her tone.

"Get into the stage. That'll afford some protection," Delwin Ferris said.

"Hitch those two horses to the front of the shaft so they can pull properly. Maybe we can still make a run for it," Fargo cut in as he started to move toward the stage. He pulled the big Sharps from its saddle holster and handed it to Ferris. "Keep an eye on that slope. Shoot if they start down," he said.

"I'm no rifleman," Delwin Ferris said.

"Give me the gun," Marge O'Day snapped and took the rifle from the man's hands. "I'll shoot the headband off the first one that moves."

"You two give me a hand," Fargo ordered Ferris and Holman and the men followed as he stepped between the shafts, started to unhitch one of the horses and bring it forward. He had just finished rehitching the horse when Marge's voice called out.

"Another one's arrived," she said and Fargo

stepped away from the stage to peer up at the top of the slope where a lone Indian had halted. The newcomer made fifteen in all, he observed silently and as he watched, the new arrival waved his arm at the others. They took a moment and then turned and retreated back into the thick tree cover.

"They're going away," Fargo heard Charity Foster say with instant hope in her voice.

"Seems they are," Pauline Beal said matter-of-factly.

"Maybe our luck's changed," Fargo said and swung onto the Ovaro. "I'm going to have a look around. The rest of you finish hitching up that other horse." He sent the Ovaro up the slope but stayed away from the heavy tree cover where the Crow had gone. He rode to the top, halted and scanned the land on the other side. He saw the spiral of dust at once and, a half-dozen yards in front of it, the double row of blue-uniformed horsemen riding across the low land. "I'll be dammed," he muttered as the cavalry platoon rode hard in a tight formation and he spurred the pinto down the slope at an angle to bring him down just ahead of the column.

The lieutenant leading the platoon waved his men to a halt as Fargo appeared and halted in his path. Young, uniform sharply creased, the lieutenant fairly exuded army discipline, spit and polish. "Lieutenant Dexter, Platoon B," the officer said. "We saw the Crow, if that's why you've come down."

"Name's Fargo, Skye Fargo," the big man said. "And that's not why I came down. There's a stage with troubles just over the hill. I know they'd welcome seeing you."

Lieutenant Dexter frowned in thought for a moment. "I'll talk to them," he said. "You lead." Fargo wheeled the Ovaro and cantered up the slope with the lieutenant and his platoon on his heels. When he crossed the top and moved toward the stage he saw that the other horse had been hitched in place as he'd ordered. He pulled to one side to let the lieutenant ride to a halt in front of the others.

"You are a sight for sore eyes, sir," Delwin Ferris said.

"Lieutenant Dexter, Platoon B, Seventh Cavalry. Where are you headed?" the officer questioned firmly.

"All the way north to Missoula Snow Bow," Holman answered. "But our next stop is Elkfoot."

"I can accompany you part of the way to Elkfoot," the lieutenant said.

"Part of the way?" Delwin Ferris echoed, protest gathering in his voice. "I insist you take us all the way to Elkfoot, Lieutenant."

Fargo watched the lieutenant spear Delwin Ferris with a glance that came close to contempt. "You insist?" Dexter echoed. "I'm under orders to proceed to Idaho territory without delay. The only reason I'll accompany you part of the way is because it doesn't take me out of the way until I have to swing west."

"Part of the way's better than nothing," Marge O'Day interrupted and drew a glance of cool approval from Dexter.

"I'll be with you long enough to send the Crow looking elsewhere for victims," Dexter said. "Now, everyone get on board, please. I've no time to waste. Where's your driver?"

"He left, along with the shotgun rider," Holman said.

The officer thought for a moment. "I'll have one of my men drive until I have to turn off," he said, then barked orders and a corporal from the rear of the column came forward to climb onto the stage. Fargo saw Charity Foster and the boy board first, her dark blond hair tossing from side to side as she quickly pulled herself into the coach. Delwin Ferris and his secretary were next aboard, Pauline Beal following with a spryness that belied her years.

"You riding along, big man?" the voice said and he looked down at Marge O'Day, her broad face holding more than curiosity, the hint of a smile in light-brown eyes.

"Why not? Elkfoot's on my way," Fargo said.

"Great," she said. "Maybe you'll turn out to be a kind of good-luck piece." She turned and climbed into the coach and Fargo backed the pinto as the lieutenant split the platoon, half riding ahead of the stage, the other half behind.

"Move out," Dexter called and Fargo swung off by himself, riding opposite the coach as it rolled on. He guessed they hadn't gone more than a mile when the line of bronzed horsemen appeared atop the high ridge alongside the road. The Indians hung back a little, but moved along with the coach in single file. Fargo's eyes followed the horsemen on the ridge as he rode, occasionally looking away from them as the miles rolled by. A furrow came onto his brow that stayed as he rode and the hours ticked away.

Lieutenant Dexter called a halt to rest the horses and took ten of his troopers with him in a fast gallop up to the top of the ridge. Fargo saw the bronzed figures vanish over the other side at once, and the lieutenant returned in a few minutes. "That'll help them decide to go their way," he said and waved the coach on. Fargo continued to ride off to the side alone, and after another half-mile the figures reappeared on the ridge. The lieutenant took note of their return, Fargo saw, but kept a steady pace. The Trailsman's own gaze went back to the line of single-file riders on the high ground and he felt the furrow come back to his brow.

The afternoon had grown long when the riders vanished from the ridge again and Fargo swung the Ovaro around, skirted the tail of the platoon and climbed to the ridgeline. He swept the land with a long gaze, took in a hundred details most men would miss, but saw no sign of the riders. They'd gone or were laying low and he turned back down the slope and ca ght up with the platoon as the lieutenant called a halt.

"I swing west here," Lieutenant Dexter told the faces that peered up at him as they stepped from the stage. "But the Crow have left. I don't think they'll be back."

"They weren't Crow," Fargo said.

Dexter turned a glance of faint annoyance at him. "I'm no tribal expert. Maybe they were Shoshoni or Nez Percé. Whatever they were, they've gone."

"They weren't Crow and they weren't any kind

of Indian," Fargo said and the lieutenant's eyebrows were not the only ones that lifted as the others climbed from the coach.

"Of course they were Indians. I know an Indian when I see one, whatever the tribe may be," Dexter said.

Fargo shook his head with quiet stubbornness. "No Indians," he murmured.

"They were riding Indian ponies, unshod," Dexter said.

"They were. I noted the tracks, too," Fargo agreed.

"Without saddles, most carrying bows, a few with rifles. That's typical," the lieutenant pressed.

"It is. They put on a damn good face," Fargo said. "Rode Indian file, too."

"Bronze-red skin?" Dexter said. "How do you explain that?"

"Dye from red clay can do that just fine."

"What makes you think they weren't Indians?" Pauline Beal cut in.

"Little things," Fargo said. "They rode single-file but too close on each other's heels. Indians leave space when they ride in file. They rode unshod ponies but they didn't sit their mounts the way an Indian sits his pony. They rode stiff and held their arms too far away from their bodies for an Indian."

"I'd say you were letting your imagination run away with you, Fargo," Dexter said. "Why would fifteen men be riding around like Crow?"

"Beats me," Fargo said pleasantly. "But those were no Indians."

"They've gone, that's all that matters," the lieutenant said to the others. "Good luck the rest of the way to Elkfoot." He threw a snapped salute, barked commands and led the platoon away at a fast canter. The others stared after the troop until the last of the horses vanished from sight and then slowly turned to the big man astride the magnificent Ovaro.

"You've an hour or so of daylight left," Fargo said. "I'd make the most of it if I were you."

"Will you ride trail for us?" Cyrus Holman asked.

"Till you reach Elkfoot," Fargo said.

"I thought perhaps Fargo would drive," Delwin Ferris said and again Fargo noted how the man had a way of making a statement sound like an order.

"Can't ride trail and drive. Which do you want?" Fargo asked.

"It's more important he ride trail," Holman said.

"That leaves us without a driver. I've never handled a team," Ferris said.

"Neither have I," Holman said quickly.

"I know how to drive a team, used to do it regular," Pauline Beal cut in. "But that was forty years ago. I don't think I've got the muscle for it now but I'll try."

"We'll do it together," Marge O'Day said. "I'll do the pulling, you do the directing."

"Sounds fine," the little old woman said with fire and she pulled herself up to the driver's seat. Marge O'Day followed her, took the reins in hand and Fargo watched the others start to return into the stage. Charity Foster was last to enter with the boy and the small form pulled away from her hand.

"Can I ride with you, Fargo?" the boy asked.

"No, you'll ride inside with me, Mitchell," Charity said at once. "Fargo has enough to do without you along."

"Can I, please, just for a little while, Fargo?" the boy asked again.

"It's all right with me," Fargo said and the boy burst into a squeal of delight, ran toward him with little legs churning. Fargo saw Charity Foster's angry glare as he hoisted the boy onto the saddle in front of him. "Mitchell, right?" he asked and the boy nodded. Fargo brought the Ovaro to the front of the stage, saw Marge snap the reins over the horses and the coach rolled forward.

"Lighten up on the left rein," Pauline Beal said and Marge responded. "Keep the same pull on both horses unless you're turning."

"What about curves in the road?" Marge asked.

"Most times they'll just follow the curve on their own," Pauline said. "Don't slack off too much. Always let them know you're in charge." Fargo smiled, not without admiration, and sent the Ovaro into a canter.

"How old are you, Mitchell?" Fargo asked the boy as they rode.

"Almost ten," Mitchell Blake answered and then, with a twinge of disappointment in his voice added, "Most folks think I'm seven because I'm small. I hate being small."

"You'll grow. Small doesn't count much, anyway. Smart is what counts," Fargo said.

He saw the boy look up at him, a long, thoughtful glance. "I guess you'd know," Mitchell Blake said. "You're big and smart."

"Some folks wouldn't agree with you on the last

part." Fargo laughed. "What brings you out here on that stage, Mitchell?"

"I'm going to visit my grandpa," Mitchell said as Fargo leveled the Ovaro off on a small plateau that let him see the road below.

"Pretty wild country up in Snow Bow. You visit him often?" Fargo queried.

"First time ever. I only saw him once back in Colorado when I was little," the boy said and let out a yelp of delight as Fargo leapt the Ovaro over a fallen log.

"How come your ma and pa didn't come along?" Fargo asked.

"Pa died a while back and Ma's hardly ever around. Charity's in charge of me and she's awful," Mitchell snapped.

"Awful how?" Fargo asked.

"She's so bossy. She never wants me to do anything that's fun. I can't play games, or hide-and-seek, or I spy, or stickball. She gets mad when I climb high trees or dive in the pond back home."

"Some people are like that," Fargo said, unable to come up with anything simple the boy could understand.

"I hope Grandpa fires her," Mitchell muttered and followed with a cry of delight as the stagecoach came into sight below. "There they are," he shouted. "This is fun."

Fargo let Mitchell enjoy himself watching the coach below but his own eyes grew narrow as he gazed back along the high ridge on the other side of the road. The line of bronzed figures had reappeared and he saw them hang back as they followed the coach below. Dusk was beginning to settle itself over the land like a scarf of purple gauze and he took the pinto through a narrow pass downward between twin rows of blue spruce, much to Mitchell's delight. He emerged on the road below just as the stage rounded a curve and Marge pulled back on the reins to bring the coach to a halt.

"That's it, even pull," Pauline said. "Very good." Her snapping blue eyes danced in her lined face as she turned them on Fargo. "We make a pretty good team, wouldn't you say, big man?" Marge O'Day's low laugh echoed Pauline's sentiments.

"Looks that way," Fargo agreed. The riders on the high ridge were still back out of sight and Fargo decided to say nothing yet about their return. He swung Mitchell down to the ground and the boy looked up happily.

"Thanks, Fargo. Can I ride with you again sometime?" he asked.

"Why not?" Fargo said and watched the boy run to the stage where Charity opened the door for him, her face set. "I'll find us a place to camp. It'll be dark in another half hour." Fargo spurred the pinto on along the road. He passed two places that would ordinarily have sufficed, kept on as the dusk grew darker and finally reined up at a small clearing surrounded on three sides by thick box elder. He was out of the saddle when Marge rolled the stage into the small clearing, put on the hand brake and the others spilled from the coach. He saw Charity come toward him with firm strides, her slender figure swaying, breasts bouncing as she dug heels into the ground.

"In the future, I'll thank you not to interfere when I tell Mitchell he can't do something," she snapped.

"I didn't interfere. I just said it was all right with me," Fargo answered.

"That was playing into his hands," she returned.

"That was telling the truth," Fargo said.

"Mitchell requires a very firm hand," Charity said stiffly.

"He doesn't seem a bad kid to me," Fargo said.

"He's headstrong, stubborn and he doesn't listen properly. I was hired to see he stays a properly mannered boy. He's very difficult to handle," Charity said tightly.

"He's not too happy with you, either. Maybe you ought to try a different approach with him," Fargo said.

"I hardly think you're an authority on child-raising." She made no attempt to hide the contempt in her voice.

Fargo allowed a slow smile. "I know one thing. Whether it's horses, women or kids, each takes its own handling. You've got to know when to go heavy and when to go light, when to shout and when to whisper, when to bear down and when to slack off. Most of all, you can't keep a smothering hand on anything with spirit."

"I'm not trying to smother the boy," Charity Foster shot back with too much anger.

"Sometimes you do things because you want to; sometimes because you just don't know any better," Fargo said. "You can decide which you fit."

"I don't fit either," Charity snapped. "And this conversation is at an end."

She spun and he walked behind her as she started back to the stage in the last of the dusk. "Maybe it was kind of pointless, anyway," Fargo said and something in his voice made her look back at him. He nodded toward the distant ridge and she followed his gaze and gasped softly. Fargo saw the others turn, peer up to where the line of horsemen had come into view.

"Good God," Delwin Ferris breathed. "They've come back?"

"Been back for a while," Fargo said. As he squinted up at the ridge, the line of horsemen slowly turned and rode back out of sight as night fell.

"You still say they're not Indians?" Holman blurted.

"That's right," Fargo said.

"I'll go along with Lieutenant Dexter," Ferris put in.

"I'll go along with Fargo," Pauline Beal snapped.

Fargo turned and swung onto the Ovaro. "Where are you going?" Marge O'Day asked.

"To check on myself," Fargo said. "I'll be back." He sent the pinto from the clearing and up the slope, rode slowly and let the night grow deeper. When he reached the high ridge he brought the horse to a walk as he headed back the way the horsemen had gone. They'd not be too far, he was certain. They'd stay close enough to move when the morning came, and when he'd gone another hundred yards or so he swung from the pinto, dropping the reins across the purple-red fruits of a coralberry shrub.

He went forward on foot in a low, loping crouch, halted after another dozen yards and dropped to one knee. The half-moon outlined a row of horses tethered together and Fargo froze. He drew his breath through lips that had become tight slits, staying motionless, and realized he was more than close enough and wiped suddenly perspiring palms on his jeans. The narrow ridge would allow little room for hurried flight, he knew grimly and he remained still and silent as a chuckwalla on a rock. The soft night wind blew across the ridge and he let his nostrils flare, drawing in deep drafts of air. Finally he rose to a crouch and, testing each step, he began to back down the ridge. Each step was a slow, careful motion and the short distance to the Ovaro seemed to take all night but finally he reached the horse, lifted the reins from the coralberry and climbed into the saddle.

He rode slowly as he moved down the slope and the moon had pulled itself half across the sky when he reached the clearing and saw the figures emerge from the stage at once, questions stark in each pair of eyes. "No Indians," Fargo said as he slid to the ground.

"You saw them?" Holman questioned.

"No," Fargo said.

"If you didn't see anything you're still only guessing," Delwin Ferris admonished.

"It's not what I didn't see, it's what I didn't smell," Fargo said and drew a collection of frowns. "I didn't smell Indian," he said. "I was close enough and I didn't smell sweat made of antelope and pemmican. I didn't smell fish oil and bear grease. I didn't smell any kind of Indian."

"This is preposterous, all of it," Ferris said. "Why would a band of fake Crows be following us?"

Fargo's eyes moved across the figures in front of him. "I thought maybe one of you could answer that," he said.

Protest flooded Ferris's face at once. "Well, I certainly can't," he said and Fargo saw Myrna Sayres's eyes meet his own with cool disdain.

"You don't expect *I* can explain that, do you?" she said.

"I can't give you any reason," Holman cut in hastily and Fargo's eyes stayed on the round, slightly puffy face for a moment before moving to Pauline Beal. The old lady's bright blue eyes held an almost mischievous glint.

"Wish I knew why anyone would be coming after me. At my age I'd be happy to admit it," she said.

"Sorry, no answers here," Marge O'Day said and Fargo saw her broad, earthy face turn away from his gaze. Fargo turned to look at Charity Foster, the boy beside her.

"I don't even think I need to comment," she said with lofty disdain. Fargo swept all of them with another slow glance. It had been a brief exchange and he hadn't really expected anything from it.

"We can't just wait here to be slaughtered," Ferris said.

"The horses can't go any farther without a night's rest. Besides, there'll be no attack till dawn. They're making like Crow and that's what the Crow would do," Fargo said. "You all settle down while I do some thinking." He turned away and strode to the far edge of the clearing, settled himself on the ground against a tree trunk and put his head back, let his eyes close. He let thoughts drift in their own pace through his mind, let bits and pieces float idly to find their own place. When he finally shut off his thoughts his mouth was a thin line across the intense, chiseled handsomeness of his face. Only a dozen hours ago he'd been enjoying a refreshing swim in a spring-fed pond and now he was a target for slaughter. A bitter sound escaped his lips at the thought.

Staying alive come morning meant pitting a makeshift masquerade against a carefully planned one. Yet there was always a chance it might work. The best-laid plans often came apart while ones put together with spit and shoe polish held fast. He pushed to his feet and strode back to the stage and waited as the others came out. "You've all traveling bags with extra clothes, I expect," he said and they nodded. "Get out your clothes, especially hats," he said and directed a glance at Charity. "That includes clothes for the boy, too," he ordered. "Meanwhile, you come with me, Mitchell. We've got to scout around for some wood."

"Yes, sir, Fargo," the boy said eagerly and half-ran to his side.

"I want a special kind of wood, Mitchell. Old logs, stumps, anything about four feet long and about round as your body," Fargo said. "Look in around the edge of the trees on that side. I'll take the other." He paused, watched Mitchell hurry away and then strode to the other side of the clearing where he began to push through brush and dig under bushes. He finally gathered five lengths of old logs and Mitchell came forward with two more, just enough to go around. He dragged the logs to the stage, where the others waited with their extra clothes in hand.

He started with Cyrus Holman's clothes first, and Marge O'Day came forward to help when she saw what he was creating. He worked with deliberate haste and the moon had carried down almost to the horizon line when he halted, stepped back and surveyed the scene with a critical eye. Seven fully clothed figures seemed to sleep around the big Brewster roadcoach. He had placed the figures of Charity and Mitchell close together beside the front wheels of the coach, two more figures half-under the main body of the vehicle and the other three alongside the rear wheels. Each length of log had been put inside clothing, made to look like figures replete with shoes and carefully positioned legs. Heads fashioned of wadded shirts and blouses were carefully covered with hats and bonnets. Even from only a few feet away the results were good, the sleeping figures recognizably those who rode the stage, and Fargo let a grunt of satisfaction pass his lips. Only a close inspection would reveal the dummy forms for what they were. If things went the way he expected they would he'd be able to prevent detection, Fargo vowed. He turned to the seven figures that stood nearby, waiting and watching. "Into the trees. It'll be dawn in an hour," he said.

"I haven't had any sleep. I don't know what's keeping me awake," Myrna Sayres protested.

"Fear," Fargo snapped and pushed his way into the thick forest where the brush grew high. He paused to let the others catch up and halted only a dozen yards from the edge of the clearing. "Stay down and stay quiet," Fargo ordered and he watched as they settled into the thickness of the high brush. He lowered himself beside Mitchell and Charity. "You were a real help, Mitchell," he said and the boy beamed. "You keep your head down come morning," he added and Mitchell nodded. Fargo shifted position and drew a glance from Charity.

"What if they realize they've been shooting at dummy figures?" she asked.

"Then your trip might be over," Fargo said and he watched her mouth tighten. He stayed quiet as the dawn came on long ribbons of pink that stretched across the sky. As the dawn gray turned to pink, he heard the sound of hoofbeats and raised himself on one knee as he unholstered the big Colt. Through the brush, he saw the riders appear, coming hard down the slope from the ridge in a concentrated charge. They poured arrows and gunfire into what seemed sleeping figures as they circled the stagecoach, completed one circle of furious fire and started the second when Fargo lifted the Colt and fired three shots. The circling horsemen reined up at once, wheeled their mounts and he fired again and saw one rider clasp his shoulder and topple from his pony. Two others went to him immediately, lifted him onto his horse and raced away with him.

The others followed, not taking the time to glance back as they ran up the slope at a full gallop. They wanted no part of fighting that could mean leaving someone behind. They'd struck in fury, done what they'd come to do and raced away, undoubtedly certain that whoever had come onto the scene would tell of seeing a Crow raiding party race from the massacre.

"It's over," Fargo said as he holstered the Colt and pushed through the brush to the clearing. When the others came along he was beside the stage, scanning the mock figures riddled by arrows and rifle bullets. He bent down and pulled an arrow from the figure clothed in Marge O'Day's garments. "Crow markings," he said, "but put on with water paint. Real Crow markings would've been made with berry and plant dye."

"Damn," Pauline Beal said, admiration in her voice.

"All right, a clever band of varmints using a new twist, making up as Crow to cover their robbing and murdering," Delwin Ferris said.

"No," Fargo answered. "They were out to kill somebody on this stage."

"You hinted at that before and everyone here told you that was nonsense." Ferris frowned.

"One of you is lying," Fargo said calmly and heard a collective gasp of protest. "Maybe more than one of you," he added almost cheerfully.

"What makes you so sure they were after somebody on this stage, Fargo?" Marge O'Day asked.

"An ordinary band of sidewinders would've gone looking for another target when the platoon rode with you. They stayed, waited and kept after you. And that's why your driver and shotgun rider stopped where they did and when they did. It was planned, all set up. It also explains why they were so damn anxious to kill me. They couldn't leave anybody alive who saw them running," Fargo said.

"If any of this is true, why didn't they just kill whoever they were after?" Myrna Sayres asked.

"The Crow wouldn't kill just one person and this was carefully planned to make it look like a Crow attack, a massacre not a murder, with no questions afterwards," Fargo answered. He watched as the others exchanged glances suddenly filled with uncertainty and suspicion and a hard smile edged his lips. "Let's move on. Take your clothes," he said.

"They're full of holes," Myrna complained.

"You'd be full of holes if it wasn't for Fargo rigging this up," Pauline Beal snapped and began pulling her things from around the log.

"We're all exhausted. We can't go on," Myrna said.

"You'll get a chance to sleep but not here," Fargo said and pulled himself onto the Ovaro as the others slowly climbed into the coach. Marge and Pauline Beal worked the team together as the coach rolled after him from the clearing. He stayed on the road only a few minutes and led the way into the forest cover, kept moving for perhaps another half hour and called a halt where a cluster of balsams grew tall. "You can sleep here," he said. "When were you due in Elkfoot?"

"I'd guess at least twenty-four hours ago," Holman said.

Fargo considered the answer for a moment. "That fits," he said finally. "Get some sleep." He pulled his own bedroll from the horse, spread it on the ground a few yards from the stage and felt the tiredness pull at him as he stretched out. It had been a long night and the next one promised to be even longer. The attack on the stage had taken careful planning. The results wouldn't be left to chance, Fargo mused. Things had to be spelled out, put on record so's it became common knowledge and that required a follow-through at the other end. He'd be there for that much, Fargo promised himself, out of plain curiosity and the satisfaction of being right. Besides, he still owed somebody. They'd damn near killed him for their masquerade. His lips drew thin as he let sleep push away further musings, his inner alarm clock set for late afternoon.

He slept soundly and when the sun lowered itself across the sky, the coolness took command of the balsam forest at once and he woke, stretched, rose and gathered up his bedroll. He used his canteen to wash and the others came awake as they heard him stirring about. Youth and age were the first up as Mitchell tumbled from the stage with Pauline Beal next. "Are we going to get ready to trick them again, Fargo?" Mitchell asked, excitement in his young face.

"Not for now," Fargo said and put his bedroll back on the Ovaro as the others came out of the coach. "Let's roll. I figure Elkfoot's another three hours but we'll make it before dark," he said.

"Can I ride a spell with you, Fargo?" Mitchell

asked and Fargo glanced at Charity, saw her lips thin.

"I cannot tell a lie. It's still all right with me," he said blandly.

"I've no comment to make on that," Charity snapped and turned back to the stage as Mitchell ran to the Ovaro and pulled himself into the saddle. Marge took the reins on the stage with Pauline Beal beside her and Fargo moved the Ovaro north, edged toward the road but stayed inside the forest. He kept the stage threading its way through the trees and took the extra time to keep off the road.

"You take the reins for a spell," he said to Mitchell when they reached a place where the trees thinned out.

"Oh, wow," Mitchell breathed as he took the reins and held them clenched in both hands.

"Arms lower, more in front of you," Fargo instructed. "No need to squeeze the reins in two. Hold them easy but firm." He let Mitchell stay with the reins, aware the pinto would pick and thread his own way through the forest, while he scanned the forest floor with narrowed eyes. Indian pony prints crossed the bed of leaves and pine needles but none were fresh and he let the boy continue to hold the reins as they made their way north. Mitchell kept up a steady stream of questions, about cougars and wolves, Indians and trees, tracking and riding, all the wide-eyed, disconnected thoughts that made up a young boy's mind. Fargo answered each question patiently, Mitchell's chatter helping to pass the time away, but his lake-blue eyes ceaselessly swept the forest depths and probed the dark green distances.

The forests stayed quiet and the hours rolled on with the wheels of the big Brewster roadcoach until Fargo took the pinto's reins, brought the stage to the edge of the open road and called a halt. He touched Mitchell on the back and the boy slid from the saddle and half-ran, half-skipped to the coach. "You take the road from here on in," Fargo told Marge and Pauline. "Elkfoot's only ten or fifteen minutes away. I'm riding on ahead. Do what I tell you to do and maybe I can find out what this is all about."

"I'd sure like that," Pauline Beal said.

"When you reach town you can tell about your driver and shotgun rider running out on you but that's all you say. Not a word about anything else that happened," Fargo instructed. "Then you go on and do what you'd ordinarily do and I'll see to the rest."

"What I'll do is enjoy a good night's sleep in a proper bed," Myrna Sayres said from the window.

"You go to the stage depot when you roll into town," Fargo told Marge. "That's usually right near the town inn. I'll be waiting there. Look for my horse."

"Can't miss him," Marge said, nodding.

"By the way, where'd this stage hail from last?" Fargo asked.

"Crawford, Wyoming," Marge said and Fargo nodded and sent the Ovaro forward and out of the woods. On the road, he put the pinto into a gallop and soon saw the buildings of Elkfoot appear as the purple haze of dusk began to settle across the land. He slowed and rode into town at a trot and saw that Elkfoot was little different from towns like it throughout the territory. He spied the white-painted, two-story frame structure in the center of town with the overnight lodging sign hanging over the front door. A few yards from the inn he saw the stage depot with two empty mail pouches hanging from wall pegs on the side of a feed store.

A beefy-faced man with the beginnings of a paunch lounged in a stiff-backed chair beside the empty pouches. Small eyes watched the big man on the magnificent Ovaro draw to a halt.

"You the Depotmaster?" Fargo asked and the man nodded, his beefy face taking on interest and caution.

"Zeb Jonah," the man said. "What can I do for you, stranger?"

"The stage from Crawford come in yesterday?" Fargo asked, keeping his voice bland.

Zeb Jonah sat up straight and his beefy face darkened with dismay at once. "No, and it's not ever comin' in," the man said. "The Crow hit it, killed everyone on it."

Fargo chose words carefully as he frowned back at the man. "My God," he breathed. "You sure about that?"

"Of course I'm sure. I wouldn't say a thing like that unless I was," Zeb Jonah said with indignation. "Man rode in here and told me, said he'd been there. I sent a posse out but they didn't find the stage. I'll send them out again tomorrow."

"Nobody left alive?" Fargo echoed.

"Nobody, the stinkin' savages," Zeb Jonah intoned.

Fargo glanced to his left as he saw the stagecoach appear, roll toward him. He slowly returned his eyes to the Depotmaster. "I don't think you've been telling me the truth, mister," he said calmly.

The man's face darkened. "What're you talkin' about, stranger?" he growled. Fargo turned to the stage, glanced at Zeb Jonah and saw the man's beefy face darken, his jaw drop open and his small eyes bulge as he stared at the coach.

Marge brought the horses to a halt and those inside began to climb out, Charity and Mitchell first to touch the ground. Fargo's glance went back to the Depotmaster. The man's jaw still hung open and in his staring face Fargo saw more than surprise. Shock and disbelief were draped on the beefy countenance.

"They look pretty damn alive to me, mister," Fargo remarked evenly.

Zeb Jonah pulled his mouth shut finally, but continued to stare at the figures beside the stage. "I heard the Crow wiped you out," he said.

Marge returned his stare. "We're here, aren't we?" she said.

"Where's your driver?" Zeb Jonah asked.

"Good question. He and the shotgun rider up and ran off on us. What kind of men are they hiring these days?" Marge snapped.

Zeb Jonah ignored the question as he continued to stare almost in awe at the figures that pulled their bags from the coach. "You're a day late," he said.

"Had some axle trouble," Marge answered smoothly, her glance passing Fargo. "You can see to the horses and find us a new driver, can't you? You are the Depotmaster," she said with some asperity.

"I'll try," Zeb Jonah said. "I'll do my best. It might take a few days, though."

"Just get it done," Delwin Ferris cut in authoritatively. "We'll all be staying at the inn." Marge picked up her bag and followed Ferris and Myrna as they started toward the inn and Fargo's eyes stayed on Zeb Jonah. The man slowly turned to him, his face still wreathed in frowns.

"You'd better stop believing everything you hear, friend," Fargo commented and slowly rode away. He rode down the main street of town, a hard-edged smile touching his lips. Zeb Jonah hadn't simply been surprised when the stage rolled up, nor filled with concern. He'd been shaken, unable to believe his own eyes. He was involved, somehow, someway, probably as the follow-through man to spread the news. Fargo cast a glance backward. Jonah was sitting on his chair, plainly still trying to digest what he'd seen, and Fargo saw a place between an old shack and a storehouse. He steered the Ovaro into it and took up a position that let him see Jonah. As dusk faded into night, the Depotmaster got to his feet, hurried around to the rear of the building and reappeared on a thin-legged bay mare.

He sent the horse up the street at a canter and Fargo moved from the place between the structures, stayed far back as he followed the man out of town. He gave Jonah plenty of headway, the sound of the man's horse drifting back clearly in the night. When the moon rose, Fargo glimpsed the Depotmaster moving between two slopes thick with bur oak. The man rode hard now, and Fargo followed just close enough to keep him in sight. Only when Jonah passed between two tall rocks did he quicken his pace until he found a hollow of land on the other side of the rocks. He continued to follow and slowed only when the odor of a cooking fire floated to him on the night breeze. He heard the sound of the Depotmaster's horse come to a halt just beyond a bend in the hollow and at once he slowed even more as he heard the sound of angry voices.

He halted, slid from the saddle with the Colt in hand and moved around the small bend to see a ramshackle hut, the door hanging open on one hinge, the glow of firelight from inside the hut. He crept closer as Zeb Jonah's voice carried through the open doorway. "What kind of shit are you trying to give me?" he heard the Depotmaster shout. "What are you trying to pull?"

"No shit. We killed every damn one of them," Fargo heard another voice answer angrily.

"Sure, that's why they were all big as life in front of me," Zeb Jonah shot back.

"You're crazy. They were shot full of holes, all of them," the other man retorted.

"That's right. They couldn't have crawled two inches much less ride off in a stage," Fargo heard another voice agree.

"Somebody's lyin' and it's not me," Zeb Jonah said. "Where are the others?"

"They went back. We'll bring them their cut. That was the agreement," the voice answered. "We thought you were bringing the money when we saw you ride up."

"The money for what—a job you didn't do?" Jonah snapped.

"We did the job, goddammit," another voice roared. That made four men inside the hut, Fargo noted. "You tryin' to weasel out on payin' us? That'll get you killed, Jonah."

"Come into town. See for yourself," Zeb flung back. "The goddamn stage is there and so's everybody that was on it."

"Let's go. We're gonna make you eat your damn words," one of the others said and Fargo stepped back, spotted a clump of elderberry bushes and lowered himself into the thick clusters of flat-topped flowers. He watched the figures stream out of the hut, Zeb Jonah in the lead, let them all come out into the open before he lifted his voice.

"Stay right there and nobody gets hurt." Jonah and the man behind him froze but the other two spun and yanked at their guns. The Colt in Fargo's hand barked twice and both men seemed to perform a strange little dance of staggered steps before they fell to the ground. But precious seconds had been used and Fargo saw Zeb and the other man dive into the trees alongside the hut. He flung himself sideways as a volley of shots tore through the elderberry bushes, came up on one knee, the Colt ready to fire again. The two men had halted inside the brush and tree cover, waiting, and Fargo drew back behind the trunk of an oak. "Give me some answers and you can walk away," he called.

The reply was a quick shot wide of its mark.

Fargo stayed silent, listened. His wild-creature hearing picked up tiny sounds, the movement of a foot, breathing that was harsh and tense. But they were playing a waiting game, hoping he'd make the first mistake. Fargo, his lips drawn tight, moved from behind the oak on steps silent as a cougar's prowl. Staying in the trees, he began to move along the edge of the open area toward the two men, pressing each footstep slowly into the ground so that there was no sharp crack of a twig, no sound of grass or brush being moved. He moved with aching slowness and heard whispered voices as he neared the two. The whispers ended and the thick brush erupted with sudden sound, leaves being brushed back, thin branches pushed aside. The sound came to him from two places. *Damn*, he swore silently. They had decided to make a break for it and split in two directions, aware he could only follow one of them. He chose the figure to his right where he'd last seen Zeb Jonah, stayed low and plunged through the high brush after his quarry.

He glimpsed the man rise to a crouch as he ran. He raised the Colt, then pulled the gun down. He wanted answers not corpses. He broke into a run, glanced back to see the dark form of the other man racing for the horses and he cursed again inwardly. Driving long, powerful legs through the brush, he quickly gained on the fleeing figure before him, drew close enough to see Jonah as the man slowed, his incipient paunch an anchor of flab to drag along. Jonah stopped, whirled, drawing in deep gulps of air as he pulled his gun out and fired at the figure coming at him through the brush. Fargo dropped to one knee as three bullets flew over his head, came forward again, every muscle poised to drop or dive away. He saw Jonah aim the gun again and was diving down as the second volley of three shots tore over his head.

He rose and charged forward as Jonah attempted to reload, dropped a bullet and looked up to see the Trailsman roar out of the brush. Fargo bowled into him swinging, felt a left hook connect with the man's jaw and Jonah went backward, trying to bring the gun up to use as a hammer when a right slammed into his cheekbone. The Depotmaster went down on one knee and the gun dropped from his hand. Fargo took a half-step backward as Jonah started to push to his feet, and he sent a long, low left hook arching upward. The blow hit the man on the point of the jaw and he almost catapulted backward, hit the ground and groaned. He half-rolled on his side, attempted to get up and fell back down again.

Fargo stepped over to him, rolled him on his back and yanked him up by the shirtfront, held him there as the man's eyes pulled open and he took a moment to focus. "I want some answers, mister," Fargo growled. Zeb Jonah blinked his small eyes and Fargo let go of his shirt, stepped back and waited as the man pushed to his feet. "What the hell is this fancy masquerade all about?" Fargo barked.

"I don't know," Jonah glowered.

Fargo's left shot out as though it were a small thunderbolt and spun Zeb Jonah completely around before he went down in a heap. Fargo waited until the man rose on his elbows and shook his head to clear it. "I'll try again. Who were they after on the stage?" he said.

"I don't know," Jonah said.

"You want to do it the hard way?" Fargo said as he stepped in, yanked the man up to his feet and twisted aside as Jonah tried a wild, swinging left. He brought up a short, stiff-armed uppercut and Jonah's head snapped back as he went down. "Answers, goddammit," Fargo roared.

Zeb Jonah lifted his head, blinked. "I don't know anything," he gasped out. "None of us did."

Fargo saw the pain and fear in the man's face as Zeb Jonah drew in long, harsh breaths. There was no steel in the beefy face, no real strength in the small eyes. Jonah could be a bully but little more. He definitely wasn't the martyr kind. "Lay it out for me while you can still talk," Fargo said.

"We were hired to makeup as Crows and wipe out the stage," Jonah said. "That's all anybody knew."

"Who hired you?" Fargo asked.

"He never gave a name."

"Bullshit," Fargo barked and as he took a step forward the man flinched. "This wasn't put together overnight. It took a lot to make it work. He had to use a name."

"He told us to call him mister," the man answered. "He was just followin' orders, anyway."

"How do you know that?" Fargo questioned.

"He'd come with orders, how to make up as Crow, how to paint the arrows, where to pick up the stage. Sometimes he'd hand out some advance money but whenever we asked somethin' special he had to go back and get more orders," Jonah said.

"He mention anyone else?" Fargo queried. Jonah glowered, fell silent and Fargo's voice took on a steel-blade edge. "You hold back on me and I'll make you into cowshit," he warned. "Give me a name."

"Tex. He mentioned Tex twice, kind of slipped out on him," the Depotmaster said.

"Tex?" Fargo echoed and Jonah nodded. "That's a lot of help," Fargo grunted.

"That's all he said." Jonah shrugged.

"And all you and the others were told was to wipe out that stage and make it look like a Crow massacre," Fargo reviewed. "No reasons, no explaining anything."

"That's right," Jonah said.

"You expect me to buy that?" Fargo pushed at the man and saw the fear behind Jonah's truculent defensiveness.

"You can buy whatever you want. It's the truth," the man muttered but it was hollow bravado, fear still stark in the depths of his small eyes. Chances were that he was telling the truth, Fargo decided. The operation had been carefully planned and carefully detailed, all aimed at hiding the truth. It was unlikely that whoever was behind it would tell anything important to a collection of hired guns. But Fargo pulled Jonah by the shoulder and spun him around roughly, unwilling to let the man pick up his thoughts.

"I'll think on this some more," Fargo growled. "Meanwhile, I'm holding on to you." He propelled the man toward the horses, let him walk on alone as he veered off to retrieve the Ovaro. "Mount up," he ordered and watched Jonah go to the thin-legged bay. He swung up onto the Ovaro when he caught the sound of a metal clasp against leather. He spun in the saddle and saw Jonah yank the six-gun from his saddlebag. Fargo flung himself from the horse as the first shot missed him by inches, hit the ground and rolled as two more shots slammed into the earth behind him. He twisted, threw himself behind the Ovaro as he drew the Colt and leaped to his feet. His shot barely cleared the saddle of the Ovaro in front of him and he saw Zeb Jonah duck down, wheel his horse around to race away. Fargo steadied his arm against the pinto's rump, fired again and Jonah toppled from the galloping horse, a red stain spreading across the back of his shirt before he hit the ground.

"Damn," Fargo swore softly. It was unlikely Zeb Jonah had anything more to reveal but if he did it died with him. Fargo climbed onto the horse and rode away unhurriedly, passed through the hollow of land and headed across the slopes. One had gotten away, Fargo reminded himself, and he'd no doubt race to tell whatever others were holed up waiting. Whoever was behind it would soon learn it had all gone wrong. With the elaborate masquerade ripped away, the attempt to disguise murder as massacre had failed. Would it mean giving up? Or just a change in plans, Fargo wondered. He had really found out only one thing. Someone was willing to kill seven people to get one. That meant high stakes and an icy, ruthless determination.

He slowed the pinto as the dark streets of Elkfoot came into view. The night had grown deep, the town asleep except for the sounds that still drifted from the dance hall as he rode past. Fargo felt the weariness flood over him as he halted outside the inn, tethered the Ovaro and woke the desk clerk, a small, elderly man in shirtsleeves and striped suspenders. Fargo took a room on the ground floor, shed his clothes and put his gunbelt on the chair beside the brass bed. He stretched out naked, on his stomach. He'd tell the others tomorrow, not so much what he had learned but what he had confirmed. They could decide what to do then, each for themselves. This was where he got off. He didn't believe in taking on big trouble when it was all spelled out by name. Besides, Joe Mellon up Beaverhead way waited to see him and Joe always had a simple job and a soft woman waiting.

Fargo turned on his side, stretched out and enjoyed the luxury of the bed. He promised himself he'd sleep late and savor every minute of it.

3

"Nobody can find the Depotmaster," Myrna snapped, irritation in her voice as she saw Fargo. He had slept late as he'd promised himself, washed and dressed leisurely and came out of his room to find Myrna alone in what served as a lobby for the inn. She wore a blue traveling suit with the neckline of the white blouse open enough to show the swell of one breast as she half-turned. An attractive woman, Fargo noted again, but spoiled and addicted to putting on airs she'd no right to put on. There were edges to Myrna Sayres's face that revealed she didn't come from the landed gentry.

"Where are the others?" Fargo asked.

"Delwin is trying to find the Depotmaster. The old lady and the woman who drove the stage went to the public stable. The little boy and his governess are in their room. I don't know where the other man is," Myrna said with a touch of disdain.

"You have a bad memory for names?" Fargo asked.

"Perhaps." She shrugged with a cool glance that

said she understood the real meaning behind the question.

"They show up, keep them here. I'll be back," Fargo told her and strolled from the inn. Elkfoot was full of mid-morning business, wagons lined up along the wide main street, miners with pack mules slowly passing along. Only the stage depot with the empty mail pouches was a quiet place and Fargo's mouth tightened as he passed it and went into the saloon. He bought a roast beef sandwich and a stein of beer to help wash down the toughness of the beef. He ate slowly, relaxed, and when he finally made his way back to the inn he found everyone waiting in the lobby. Delwin Ferris's eyes bored into him with authoritative indignation while the others were simply uneasy and waiting.

"Were you out looking for the Depotmaster?" Ferris asked.

"Nope," Fargo said. "Was out looking for a roast beef sandwich. Found one, too."

"The Depotmaster seems to have disappeared," Ferris snapped.

"He disappeared dead," Fargo said blandly and saw eyebrows go up collectively. "He was one of them. That's why he was so flabbergasted when you all rolled in last night. He'd been told you were all dead. His job was to spread the news about the massacre."

"How do you know all this?" Marge O'Day asked.

"I figured as much and I followed him out of town last night, saw him meet with some of the others," Fargo said.

"I suppose I shouldn't ask how come he's dead," Myrna said but her dark blue eyes probed into Fargo.

"He was a damfool. Damfools get themselves killed easy," Fargo replied. He let his eyes sweep the group with a long, slow glance. "Remember that," he said.

"I'll sure remember it," Pauline Beal said. "And I'll remember that if it weren't for that scheme you rigged up we'd all be dead the way they wanted us to be."

"I'm sure we all appreciate that," Delwin Ferris said and managed to make the remark sound like a dismissal. He focused his glance on the big man and let his lips purse for a moment. "We haven't thought about what we're going to do yet. Of course, I'm going on somehow, someway. We'd like you to wait around a while longer," he said.

"Why?" Fargo asked casually.

"We will need two more horses if we decide to go on. Perhaps you could pick two out for us," the man said.

Fargo shrugged. "I want to rest my Ovaro another day and give him a grooming. I'll be around till morning," he said and Ferris nodded with satisfaction. Fargo turned, started to walk from the lobby when Mitchell called out.

"Where are you going, Fargo? Can I come along?" the boy asked.

"I'm sure Fargo has things to do alone," Charity said quickly. "You're staying right here with me, Mitchell."

Fargo saw the boy's face mirror hope and dismay. "Maybe later, Mitchell," he said and strode quickly away, unwilling to weaken Charity's authority too much. The boy was her responsibility, no matter how she handled him.

He strode out to the Ovaro, swung onto the horse and rode from town, took a slope that led him into high ground and he swept the land south beyond Elkfoot with a long, slow survey. He didn't expect trouble, not this soon. The scheme had blown up. It'd take a while to put together something else. His eyes moved north across the land and he caught the distant sparkle of blue under the bright sun where the Missouri River headwaters gathered. Powerful, rich and lush country, soft yet savage. Crow country, he grunted silently. There were myriad ways through it, none of them easy and all of them dangerous. But it was beautiful land to ride, filled with all that nourished the spirit as well as the body. It was country that was good for the soul, if not the scalp.

He moved the Ovaro on unhurriedly, explored a low hill and dismounted to enjoy a field of alpine fireweed, went on finally and let the Ovaro drink from a cold, clear stream. He finished the remainder of the afternoon relaxed under a big Utah white oak and enjoyed the leisure of the day. The peace helped to wipe away the events of the last forty-eight hours. Cold-blooded murder was always a rotten business. Massacres were pure savagery. But murder disguised as massacre left a particularly sour taste in his mouth and as he rode back to Elkfoot he looked forward to getting an early start come morning.

When he reached town, he took the Ovaro into

the public stable where a man with a limp gazed at the horse in admiration. "Give him a box stall. I'll be in to groom him later tonight," Fargo said.

"The best one we have. Don't get many like him in here," the man said as he led the Ovaro away. Fargo walked from the stable to the inn, where he saw Pauline Beal sitting on the front porch. She quickly rose as she saw him.

"I'm to call the others," she said and hurried inside. Fargo went into the lobby, leaned against a mantelpiece and saw Marge O'Day come in first. She'd put on a brown dress with a full skirt that hid the fifteen or so pounds extra she carried but let her big bust push over the top of a square neckline.

"It's almost dark. I wondered if maybe you'd changed your mind and decided just to go," she said with a slightly cynical grin. The lobby lamp hadn't been lighted yet and the dusk took the edge of hardness from Marge's broad face and left a high-cheekboned, strong attractiveness.

"I said I'd stay," he answered with a touch of reproof.

She tossed him a broad smile. "You did, and I should've known better," she said. "You're not the usual kind." She paused, started to add more but pulled back words as Cyrus Holman came into the lobby with the others close on his heels. They made a semicircle with Charity and Mitchell at the far right. He nodded back as Mitchell waved almost shyly at him and Delwin Ferris stepped forward, cleared his throat.

"We've reached a decision. It's very important to

each of us that we go on to Missoula Snow Bow. We paid good money for a stagecoach to take us there. We'll take things into our own hands and go on. It's owed us," Ferris said. "We want you to take us through. We'll share the cost of hiring you. Five hundred dollars, Fargo. That's a lot of money."

"For most things. Not for being a target," Fargo said.

"You won't be a target. They failed, whoever they were. It's over," the man said.

"I'd say anybody who went to all the trouble to rig that fake Crow attack isn't about to just give up," Fargo said.

"I say it's over," Ferris snapped. "Will you take us through?"

"Sorry, no deal," Fargo said. "You're fools if you try to take that stage through Crow country, even if nobody was after you."

"We've no choice. Everyone here has their own reasons. They all add up to getting to Snow Bow," Ferris said. "Six hundred, the money in your hand."

"With you, we've got a chance. Without you, we've damn little chance," Marge O'Day put in. "I asked around about you. You're the very best."

"And I intend to stay alive," Fargo said. "I don't need money for a fancy casket."

Charity Foster's voice cut in, each word chipped out of ice. "We're wasting breath. Mister Fargo doesn't care what happens to us any longer. He puts limits on helping," she snapped.

"He puts limits on being a damfool," Fargo returned.

"And on human decency and responsibility to others," she flung back acidly.

"Now, there's no need for harshness," Delwin Ferris cut in hastily, his voice soothing as he turned his gaze on the big man. "Will you give yourself the night to think about our offer?" he asked.

"Why not?" Fargo shrugged. "But don't expect anything different. I'll start thinking about it while I groom my horse." He strode out of the room and into the night that had settled down outside. Maybe they'd come to their sense by morning, he muttered silently, though he didn't put much store in that happening. They were all desperate to get to Snow Bow and desperation made for damfools. He pushed aside thoughts of the others as he arrived at the stable and went into the big roomy box stall where the Ovaro greeted him with a toss of its jet-black head.

He had a dandy brush, curry and hoof pick in his saddlebag and the stableman supplied him with a stable sponge. Grooming the horse was always as much a pleasure as a task. Even on the trail he took time to use a sweat scraper. A properly cared for horse worked better, responded better and deserved its grooming. Fargo set to rubbing down the Ovaro, working with unhurried care and he'd just finished using the stable sponge when he saw the small figure appear in the doorway of the stall, clad in a long nightshirt. "Aren't you supposed to be in bed?" Fargo frowned.

"Charity's asleep. I sneaked out," the boy said.

"What are you doing down here?" Fargo asked as

he put the stable sponge down and Mitchell took a few tentative steps into the stall.

"I had to come see you. I'm sorry about the way Charity talked to you. I wanted you to know I think she's wrong and she's mean," Mitchell explained.

"Thanks," Fargo said and met the boy's wide-eyed seriousness gravely. "Sometimes, when people are scared and angry they say a lot of things they shouldn't say. Charity was both."

"She was rotten mean to you and I hate her," Mitchell said. "Can you take me with you, Fargo?"

"Whoa, there, slow down," Fargo said.

"They all decided to go on no matter what. When I said they ought to listen to you they told me little boys should be seen and not heard. I want you to take me to my grandpa, Fargo."

"Charity would never agree to that," Fargo said.

"I don't care. I'm sure Grandpa would pay you when we got there," Mitchell said.

"It's not that. Charity's your governess. You're in her care. I just can't go running off with you. She could have the marhsal after me."

"I don't care what she does," Mitchell said with a ten-year-old's singular determination. He bolted forward suddenly, buried himself against Fargo's long legs. "I'm scared, Fargo. I know you're right. They'll just get themselves killed and me with them and I'll never get to see my grandpa."

Fargo's hand pressed down on the little boy's soft, tousled hair and he felt the small form trembling against him. "I won't go with them. I'll run away first chance I get," Mitchell said.

"That won't get you to your grandpa," Fargo said as Mitchell unwrapped his arm from around him.

"I won't be dead. I'll find a way," the boy answered, determination in his small face. He would try to run away, Fargo was convinced of that, and on his own he'd have all the chance of a baby chick in a den of wolves. Not that he'd have much more staying with the stage. *Damn,* Fargo muttered inwardly. Mitchell was a victim of adult stupidity, selfishness and maybe greed. He wasn't different from a lot of kids in that but Mitchell's young life would pay the price in this instance and Fargo swore. That was wrong. "Damn," he said again, aloud this time.

"I'm sorry I bothered you, Fargo. I guess I was thinking wrong about everything," Mitchell said. "I'd better get back before Charity wakes up." Fargo watched the small nightshirted form turn, the smooth, young face trying hard to hide its disappointment.

"Wait," Fargo called out. "I've been thinking. I haven't been in the north country in some while and your grandpa's expecting you. Might as well take the stage through."

"Wow," Mitchell shouted and leaped forward. Fargo caught him in his arms and lowered him to the ground. "Thanks, Fargo, thanks," Mitchell said as he clung with all the strength of his little body.

"This is just between us, Mitchell," Fargo said. "Not a word to any of the others. So far as they know, I'm just taking their deal."

"Just between us," Mitchell said, happy to be a conspirator.

Fargo took the boy by the shoulders, his face grave. "One thing more, Mitchell. It'll be hard and dangerous. I can't promise we'll make it. You've got to understand that," he said.

"We'll make it with you along, Fargo," Mitchell said with the blind trust of the very young. Another hug and the small figure dashed into the night. Fargo returned to continue grooming the pinto, finished with the hoof pick and put his things away. He walked slowly back to the inn through the still darkness and undressed in the room and lay across the bed, unsure whether he cursed himself for being softheaded or softhearted.

He lay awake as thoughts slowly paraded across his mind. If he'd any chance of making it he had to find out the truth about everybody on the stage. He'd pull it from them, in his own way and his own time, in any way he could. If he was going to be a target he wanted to know why. That could spell the difference between living and dying and he wasn't about to take the second option. His idling thoughts broke off as he heard footsteps at the door, soft, shuffling. His hand closed around the butt of the Colt when the knock came, a barely audible sound. He rose, silently pulled on trousers and moved toward the door. He paused, listened. The footsteps had halted with the knock.

Fargo, the gun still in his hand, unlatched the door and stepped back. Moonlight from the window caught the figure that slipped into the room, touched the high cheekbones of the broad face and glinted on the made-blond hair. Marge O'Day turned, found him as she closed the door and he saw she wore a nightdress that hung straight from her wide shoulders, pushed out where it touched the large breasts.

"Surprised?" she asked with a hint of laughter in her voice.

"I'd say that," Fargo admitted. "This a social call or did they send you?"

"Strictly on my own," Marge O'Day said as her light brown eyes moved across the beauty of his powerfully muscled shoulders and traveled down across the firm pectoral contours and the hard, flat stomach.

"You've a reason," Fargo said. "Company or convincing?"

"Both, I guess," Marge replied. "I won't waste words, Fargo."

"Good," the big man said.

"Money didn't do it with you. I thought maybe something else might," Marge O'Day said.

"You that desperate?" Fargo asked.

"I've no place to go back to. Going on is all there is for me. I guess that makes me desperate," she said.

"I'm listening," Fargo said.

Marge O'Day turned to fully face him and her hand lifted, began to undo a row of buttons that went down the front of the nightdress. When she reached those at her waist, the top of the dress fell open, slipped from her shoulders and cascaded to the floor and Marge O'Day stood naked before him. Fargo took in a throbbingly earthy body, full and rich, the added weight not enough to take away from the lushness of it, large breasts that still avoided sagging, each tipped by a surprisingly small, brown-pink nipple and brown-pink circle. Marge O'Day's belly curved outward in a convex little mound, the wide hips made a little wider by extra pounds but her full legs firm, thighs round and without flab, tapering down to calves that retained their thinness. Below the convex belly a bushy, dense triangle formed a curly nap that completely fit her full figure.

"You like what you see?" Marge asked.

"Yes, you're still a lot of woman, Marge O'Day," Fargo said.

"It's yours, whenever and wherever, if you take us through," she said.

Fargo's smile was slow. "Showing's one thing. Proving's another," he said.

"So it is," Marge said and she stepped forward, pressed her mouth over his, her lips wide, soft and wet. Her body came against his and he felt the softness of the large, pillowy breasts against his chest. He felt her lips move on his mouth, draw him in and her tongue glided slowly, flicked back, a promise and a call. Fargo felt Marge's hands on his trousers, pulling open buttons until the garment fell down to the floor. But he was already responding to her touch and his own near-rigid warmth came up to push against her thighs. "Oh, Jesus," Marge breathed and fell back onto the bed, pulling him with her. His face buried itself into the two large, down-soft mounds and he brushed his lips across the two brown-pink nipples that had already grown firm.

Marge's thighs fell open and he could feel the warmth of them as they came together against his legs, held for a moment and then fell open again. Her wide hips lifted, beckoned, but he held back and pulled first one large breast into his mouth, then the other. Marge made small groaning sounds but the down-soft, pillowy breasts were not her prime areas of sensitivity, he realized when he moved his hand down across the convex belly and through the dense and curly nap. "Ah, ah, Jesus," Marge burst out in a sudden explosion at his touch. The pillowy breasts jiggled against him as a shudder ran through her and her wide hips lifted to meet his hand. He slid his fingers downward, through the curly tendrils and still farther down as Marge let out a low, quivering groan of pleasure. The sound became almost a throaty laugh as he touched the soft, wet opening, probed inside and Marge brought one hand up to push against his, pressing his deeper into her. "God, oh, yes, go on . . . go on, go on," she murmured between groans and he saw her eyes were closed, her wide mouth parted. "Ah, ah . . . ah, Jesus, more," Marge cried out and her hands yanked at him.

He lifted, slid his pulsating warmth against her belly and Marge gasped out in delight, lifted, rubbed and again he heard almost a throaty laugh of pure delight. He drew back, brought his own male eagerness to her and slid effortlessly into the smooth, wet, welcoming avenue. "Ah, Jesus . . . ah, ah, good, good," Marge murmured, clasped her full-fleshed thighs around him as she reached arms up and pulled his face down into the pillowy mounds. She held him there between their downy softness as her wide hips began to move with him, draw in, push forward, draw back again and come forward once more. Marge took on a slow, easy movement that at other times would have been languorous but a short, quick thrust at the end of each motion carried the intensity of hard-edged pleasure.

Fargo stayed with her, began to quicken the pace and let himself thrust deeper, felt the flesh of her thighs against him quiver as she groaned in pleasure. Marge O'Day's full, wide hips were a saddle of comfort and the big, pillowy breasts, the fullness of her earthy body encompassing, surrounding, making the world a place of flesh, touch and absolute gratification. Long, low, sounds came from deep inside her, a kind of music of the senses, ecstasy given voice. "Ah, aaaaah, ah, ah, yes, yes . . . aaaah," Marge groaned and groaned again, each sound one of exhortation and approval. No novice to passion, Marge knew how to measure ecstasy, cling to joy and prolong the exquisite. Fargo's lips found hers, stayed with her as tongues met, caressed, slid alongside each other and he felt the heat of her pleasure. He continued to press deep inside her, back and forth, each long slow thrust more pleasurable than the one before and suddenly he felt the pillow breasts begin to jiggle against him. Marge's full body lifted, pressed hard into him. "Yes, now, ah, ah, Jesus, big man, Jesus," she gasped and her thighs clamped around him with quivering warmth.

He felt her seem to expand under him, groan with the deep sound of pleasure beyond the holding and she clung until her body relaxed with a deep, groaning sigh and her legs fell open from around him. She slumped back onto the bed and pulled him with her and her wide mouth formed a smile of contentment.

"Good enough proving?" she slid at him.

"Good enough," Fargo said and Marge pushed herself to a sitting position and Fargo watched the large breasts sway gently.

"You were something special, big man, but I expected that," she said and leaned forward, let her breasts push against his chest.

"The voice of experience?" Fargo laughed.

"Enough," Marge said. "Though not in recent times. I've been running things for the last few years. Manager, madam, house mother, whatever name you want to give it. But I still know a good man when I see one." She fell silent, her eyes on him and he leaned on one elbow and brushed his hand across one large breast and enjoyed its downy softness. "Well?" she said. "You going to make me wait till morning for an answer?"

"No." Fargo smiled. "No sense in that. I'll ride trail for you."

"Great," Marge said and flung her arms around him. "I guess I did the right thing by deciding to pay you a visit."

"Depends on how you look at it," Fargo said blandly.

"Meaning what?" Marge frowned as she pulled back.

"I'd decided to take the deal before you came calling," Fargo said mildly and saw the frown come across Marge's brow. She stared at him for a long moment as the frown deepened.

"You bastard," she breathed softly. He let himself look hurt. "You just plain took advantage of me," she accused.

"No, I just let you do what you wanted to do anyway," Fargo said.

"Bastard," Marge said again but this time her lips formed a wry smile with the word. She pulled the nightdress on and stood up.

"You taking back your offer?" Fargo asked.

"I didn't say that," Marge answered and quickly left the room. He put the lock on and fell across the bed. It was still warm from her, still smelled of her and he sighed contentedly as he closed his eyes. He'd come to know only one part of Marge O'Day. There was more, he was certain, to her and to the others. He'd be finding out before the trip ended. Something told him he'd have to if he wanted to stay alive. He slept and let the night wend its way to morning.

4

They were gathered waiting in the lobby when he came from his room in the morning. They breathed a collective sigh of relief when he told them he'd decided to take their offer but relief became something else as he barked questions. Delwin Ferris led the protest in his authoritative manner. "I resent your remarks and your attitude, Fargo," the man said. "We've all told you there's no reason anyone should be after any of us."

"Somebody is and he's going to try again. I aim to find out why before it's too late," Fargo said. "Let's talk about the stage, first. Far as I know the stage doesn't go past Elkfoot."

"They will if they get enough passengers going on. That's what happened with us and we each paid a bonus price to go on," Ferris answered.

"I want to know why each of you is on this stage. You start, Ferris," Fargo said.

"I'm going to Missoula Snow Bow to retire and Myrna's coming with me," Ferris answered.

"Retire from what?" Fargo questioned.

"I was office manager for the Abelson Shipping Company back in Missouri," Ferris said.

"Seems you're awful desperate to get to Snow Bow just to retire and sit around," Fargo commented and caught the quick glance Myrna shot at Ferris.

"A man's holding a piece of land for me. If I don't get there by a certain date he'll sell it off and I don't want that," Ferris said. Fargo nodded and kept the skepticism from his face as he wondered if the answer had been prepared or if Ferris simply thought fast. He turned to Cyrus Holman and the man licked his lips nervously.

"I'm a traveling salesman," Holman said. "Cattle feed and livestock medicine. If it's got four legs I've got something for it." He tried a quick grin with the slogan that faded into uneasiness.

"What's your damn rush to reach Snow Bow?" Fargo asked.

"Got to beat the competition. Heard there were a lot of new cattle breeders starting up there," Holman said.

"They'll have to be raising mountain goats," Fargo commented and met Marge O'Day's light brown eyes. Little glints of amusement touched their depths.

"I'm between dance halls. I was told they could use me in Snow Bow. I want to get there before some other filly does," she said and Fargo turned away without comment.

Pauline Beal's snapping blue eyes met his gaze with direct boldness. "Got an older brother there. He's been sick. I want to get there before it's too late. I'd be sorry if I didn't make it in time," she said.

Fargo nodded and Charity's voice answered before he turned to her. "I understand Mitchell has already told you he's on his way to visit his grandfather," she said.

"He didn't tell me why he has to get there in such a damn hurry," Fargo said.

"My orders are to have him there by the fifteenth of the month. I can't wait around for another stage that might never make the whole run. I took the opportunity to get on this stage," Charity said.

Fargo set her answer aside with the others and slowly scanned the group. "The attack on this stage was carefully planned. They bought the stage drivers, went to a lot of trouble to make it seem like the Crow did the killing. There's a damn good reason that doesn't fit with all your nice, reasonable explanations. One of you is lying. Maybe more than one of you. But I'll find out."

Ferris regarded him with almost tolerant amusement. "Not that I'm at all concerned, but how do you expect to do that?" he asked.

"Look when it's time to look, listen when it's time to listen and lean when it's time to lean," Fargo answered and his easy manner snapped off abruptly as he barked the next question. "Any of you know a man named Tex?" he asked and his eyes swept the others with probing sharpness. Each shrugged denial.

"Why?" Holman asked and Fargo saw only curiosity in his round face.

"Those fake Crows were given orders from a man who mentioned the name Tex twice," Fargo said. "I'd guess this Tex is the one behind everything that's happened." He watched as they shrugged again and exchanged glances that seemed honestly perplexed.

"Have you finished with your questions?" Holman asked irritatedly.

"For now," Fargo said mildly.

"I found a man who'll sell us two horses for the stage. He showed them to me yesterday. He's just at the end of town," Holman said.

"Let's go look," Fargo said. "Meanwhile, the rest of you get ready to roll." Cyrus Holman strode outside and as Fargo started to follow he found Charity at his side, Mitchell standing by.

"I must say I'm surprised. I didn't expect an overnight attack of conscience," she said.

"Don't let it go to your head, honey," Fargo growled, saw the tiny smile deep in Mitchell's eyes and strode on to where Holman waited outside. When he reached the end of town with the traveling salesman he saw a tattered corral where a half-dozen horses were penned. A man stepped from a nearby shack, nodded at Holman and went into the corral to pull two horses forward with rope halters.

"These are the two I showed you yesterday, friend," the man said and peered at Fargo out of a pair of shrewd, narrow eyes. "Give you a good price for 'em."

"Not for these two, mister," Fargo said as he took in the two horses.

"What's wrong with these two?" Holman muttered in a whisper.

"Swollen fetlocks, thin cannon bones. They'd last maybe two days pulling the stage," Fargo said and he stepped into the corral and surveyed the other horses more closely. He finally chose two with good strong rumps and solid thigh muscles and had Holman pay a fair price. He led the horses back to the stage and had them hitched in place as Marge appeared, with the others close on her heels. She and Pauline climbed onto the driver's seat.

"Four-horse team, now," Pauline said to her. "It'll take more attention and more muscle till you get the hang of it." Marge nodded and her eyes were on Fargo as he rode alongside the coach.

"Your first stop is the general store. You're all going to need food. Buy enough for a week," Fargo said. "As much easy-cooking stuff as you can."

"A week?" Holman frowned.

"Better more than less. I could get real hungry," Fargo said and rode away. He waited near the end of town until he saw the stage roll down the street, then swung onto the road from Elkfoot where it led north. He stayed on it until it curved west and the land grew wild. He paused, let the stage catch up to him and led the way up a gentle slope dotted with white fir. The two new horses were giving Marge trouble, he saw, still unruly hitched into wagon shafts. But she was holding them in line with Pauline's advice, he saw, and he called a halt in mid-afternoon.

"Can I ride with you?" Mitchell asked as he

appeared at his side. "Charity said it was all right with her."

Fargo nodded and the boy pulled himself into the saddle and simply enjoyed being there. Fargo rode on, found terrain that let the stage roll up into the high land without real trouble. But the land was growing steeper, harsher, he saw, and when night slid over the hills he took the stage into a place where the oaks grew over a rock overhang. Pauline saw to cooking some canned stew they'd bought and Fargo had the horses fed and watered before the others finished their meal. He took his bedroll down as the others prepared to sleep, Mitchell and Charity inside the coach, the others bedding down outside and close by.

He saw the tiredness lining Marge's face as she paused beside him. "It'll be easier tomorrow. The new horses will settle down," he told her.

"That's what Pauline said. I hope you're both right. I don't want this driving business to interfere with my social life," Marge said and her smile held slyness in it as she went on. Fargo took his gear into the trees and stretched out, relaxed and let his thoughts wind backward. They had all given him their stories and it was time to examine them again. He let his thoughts concentrate on Delwin Ferris, first. The man's answers had been more glib than substantial, their reasonableness all on the surface. Land was for the taking in Missoula Snow Bow. There was no reason to race through Crow country for a piece of land. Delwin Ferris was being less than honest, Fargo mused, and brought Cyrus Holman into his thoughts. A fancy dresser and salesman of cattle feed and medicines supposedly on his way to find cattle breeders where there were damn few. That didn't hold together, either. Maybe it was not a complete lie but still wasn't the truth, Fargo grunted.

Marge was next and he felt his lips draw back. Believing her would be easy. He wanted to believe the story she'd given him, he realized, but the best he could do was settle for half of it. He didn't doubt she was between dance halls but she was awfully desperate to reach someplace where they might hire her. She was putting her neck out on a possibility and Marge O'Day was too experienced and too practical for that kind of wide-eyed pursuit. It was like a dress that fitted but didn't fit right.

Pauline Beal's reasons held together best of all. Time had the kind of meaning for her it could never have for the others, more than enough to make her take risks. His thoughts went to Charity. Her desperate anxiety to reach Snow Bow seemed fashioned more of stupidity than deceit and that fitted her. She'd been given a date on which to produce Mitchell and she was determined to get him there early rather than late. But that'd be like her, proper, punctual, concerned with doing the right thing. It'd probably upset her more than Mitchell if she were late with him. Fargo smiled and set Charity aside with Pauline Beal. He paused, returned to Delwin Ferris and Myrna Sayre. He had neglected her, he realized. She'd gone along with the role of simply being Ferris's companion. Maybe she was a lot more than that, Fargo guessed. Maybe it was really Myrna who was desperate to reach Snow Bow. She had said nothing, stayed very much the shadow beside Ferris. He set Myrna Sayres aside in his mind as a very open question mark.

He closed his eyes, again hoped Marge wouldn't be one of the lies he knew lay somewhere in the stage. But he'd find out, he promised himself, one way or the other as he let sleep push away further speculation. The night stayed still and he slept well until he woke with the new day to find Mitchell up and awake ahead of him. "You figure to ride again with me?" Fargo asked and Mitchell nodded. "You ask Charity?" Fargo questioned.

"She didn't mind yesterday," Mitchell answered.

"Better ask. Today's another day," Fargo said and Mitchell made a face.

"Yeah, and you never know what she's going to be like," he grumbled. "I'll ask." He hurried back to Charity while Fargo saw to the horses and reappeared in moments. "She said all right," he called happily and climbed onto the Ovaro. Cyrus Holman paused, fastened Fargo with a faintly irritated glance.

"Wouldn't we make better time staying on the low ground?" he asked.

"We would," Fargo said as he tightened the cinch under the horse's belly.

Holman's mouth tightened. "Then why aren't we there?" he snapped.

"This is the scenic route," Fargo said. "No extra charge."

Holman sputtered but turned away and stalked back to the stage and Fargo saw Marge and Pauline Beal watching. Pauline chuckled as she walked on.

"The fool deserved that," Marge said and Pauline paused in front of the big man.

"I'm not like him. I know you've a good reason for not staying on the low ground. I just don't know what it is," she said.

"Anybody following will take longer to get to us on high land," he told her. "But mostly because of the Crow. Down there we'd be an easy target to swoop down on from anywhere. Up here it's not the same." She nodded and climbed onto the stage.

Fargo took the Ovaro out ahead with Mitchell, motioned to the stage and indicated a stretch of fairly level ground between two tree-covered slopes. He watched Marge take the coach onto the wide flat passage and sent the pinto higher into the hills. By midday he halted on a flat, high ledge and scanned the land behind them. The tracks of the stage would be easy to pick up and enough time had gone by for anyone following to start to close in. But though he scanned the very edge of the horizon he saw no signs of pursuing riders and returned his gaze to the thickly covered terrain ahead.

He glimpsed the stage below still rolling across the passageway and he sent the Ovaro through a cluster of white fir and out onto a small clear area where he reined up and peered at the marks on the ground. "Crow hunting party. They got a deer here, carried it down that way," he said to Mitchell.

"How do you know they were Crow?" Mitchell asked. " 'Cause this is Crow country?"

"Partly, though the Flathead and Nez Percé ride here, too." Fargo said. "But this hunting party had one rider with the rest on foot. The Crow like to hunt on foot more than most other tribes."

He swung back onto the Ovaro as Mitchell peered at him. "How long does it take to get to learn so much, Fargo?" Mitchell asked.

"Some people never learn," Fargo answered.

"You mean they're not smart enough?"

"It's not being smart. It's being able to become a part of everything around you, earth, wind, sky, trees, shrubs, flowers, streams, animals, birds. After that you begin to learn the rest, how nature works, how animals act, how men behave," Fargo said and paused. "All except one thing," he grunted.

"What's that?" Mitchell asked.

"Women," Fargo said. "You'll never learn how they'll behave."

"I know that already," Mitchell said. "My ma's off having a good time all the time with some boyfriend. She doesn't care what I do. That's why she hired Charity. She cares about everything I do. It's more than I can figure out."

"Don't spend too much time on it," Fargo said.

"My grandpa cares about me," Mitchell said and Fargo heard the combination of yearning and defensiveness in the boy's voice.

"I'm sure he does but I thought you told me you only saw him once," Fargo said.

"Yes, but he sends me a letter every month, real great letters, too. He wanted me to live with him after my pa died but Ma wouldn't let him. That's why he's sent for me."

"To take custody of you?" Fargo frowned.

"I don't know what exactly. He wrote that it was real important for me to come visit."

Fargo put the boy's words away in a corner of his mind. He sent the Ovaro down a narrow path inside a stand of quaking aspen and rejoined the stage as the level passage came to an end. Marge had halted where a stream coursed down through the shrubs and Pauline held a water bucket for the horses. The others had stepped from the stage to stretch.

"You ride the stage for the rest of the afternoon, Mitchell," Fargo said. "I'm going to be doing some fast, hard riding."

"Whatever you say, Fargo," Mitchell answered as he slid to the ground. Fargo turned to Marge and Pauline.

"Take the next mile or so real slow. The passage is wide enough for you but not by much. I'll meet you at the other end," he said and both women nodded soberly. He wheeled the pinto and rode upward where a steep passage curved to the right. He was out of sight of the stage in moments. He let the pinto set his own pace up the steep climb and finally emerged onto high ground flat enough to take at a canter. He had seen more than enough tracks as he'd ridden with Mitchell but he wanted more than tracks and he followed down along a stand of alder until he reined up sharply. The band of bronzed horsemen moved easily just below where he'd halted and his eyes scanned the hill across from them and saw the second band of riders. They were peering down at the stagecoach below them, for the moment more curious than threatening.

Fargo hung back and watched, moving forward as the two parties of Crow warriors exchanged hand signals and spurred their ponies on along the high ground. They left the stage below and behind as they rode on. Fargo followed, turning after them as the bands converged with the other and both headed into a wooded ravine. They disappeared into thick alders and Fargo slowed as he followed, listened and heard the sound of running water as he pushed through the trees. His nostrils flared and he drew in the odor of smoke and hides being dried. The trees thinned out and he halted as he came in sight of the camp spread out along the banks of a wide but shallow mountain river.

His eyes narrowed as he scanned the scene before him: a full camp with five tipis, hide-drying racks, squaws and kids scurrying naked across the cleared land. He saw a tall Indian with a prominent nose, an eagle's feather in a wide headband and a tomahawk with a carved handle at his waist step from the center tipi as those who had just returned gathered around him. Fargo watched as they gestured back to the forest, barked words and added a few gestures in sign language. The Crow spoke Siouan which he knew fairly well. He was too far away to hear but it was plain they were telling about the stagecoach and he saw the chief nod gravely before going back into his tent. The others dispersed, some into tipis, others to the side of the wide river and some to where squaws brought food.

Fargo slowly backed the Ovaro, turned carefully and retraced his steps until he was far enough away to put the horse into a canter. The stage was halted at the end of the passage, waiting, when he rode up. He saw the instant concern on Marge's face. "We wondered what happened to you," she said.

"Crow, all over the place," Fargo said. "The real thing, this time."

"You think they've seen us?" Holman called from the window of the coach.

"Oh, they've seen you, all right," Fargo said.

"Are they going to attack?" Myrna Sayres asked.

"I don't know," Fargo said. "They don't know what to make of a stagecoach all alone up here, which is what I was hoping might happen."

"Why?" Holman frowned.

"I knew they'd see us sooner or later. Down on the road we'd be just one more fool stage. Up here we're strange. Indians have their own ways, their own superstitions. Something out of the ordinary could be an evil omen better left alone," Fargo explained.

"And if they decide differently?" Holman pressed.

"We'll have bought some time and we'll be no worse off," Fargo said. "Now let's get a spot to camp." He led the stagecoach across a narrow, rocky path and into a space between two firs in the denseness of a thick forest as night began to lower itself over the hills. They ate cold beef jerky and when he took his bedroll, Marge paused beside him.

"You going off by yourself again?" she asked. "The shepherd watching his flock from afar?"

"Something like that." Fargo smiled, walked into the trees and felt Marge watching him until the night swallowed him up. He went on a dozen yards or so, found a spot and set his bedroll down and undressed to the bottoms of his underwear. He lay, arms behind his neck, and listened to the night sounds. A family of raccoons marched past nearby, a lone weasel farther off to his right. An almost full moon silhouetted the bats that swooped low through the trees. He'd made a wager with himself and he smiled as he heard the footsteps moving toward him, hurrying, then pausing, hurrying forward again.

"Fargo! Where the hell are you?" the whispered voice called out and he sat up.

"Walk straight ahead," he replied and saw her appear a moment later walking toward him. She halted as she reached him, the nightdress covering her full figure in the moonlight that filtered through the thickness of the leaves.

"The shepherdess coming to keep the shepherd company?" Fargo said.

"Something like that." Marge chuckled as she lifted her arms and pulled the nightdress off. She sank down atop him at once, her nakedness a soft blanket of sensuousness, the big breasts pushing down onto his face. Her hands reached down, pulled away the bottoms of his underwear and his already reaching, burgeoning maleness came up to slap against her convex soft belly as she pressed down. "Oh, Jesus, big man," Marge groaned, lifted her full-fleshed thighs and rubbed her belly up and down against him. "Oh, Jesus," she breathed and he felt the earthy, throbbing richness of her flow over and around him, her pure, unvarnished sexuality inflamed. Marge made love with him as she had that first night in the hotel, with deep, groaning sounds of pure pleasure, possessed of a raw wanting that left no time or place for subtleties. There was no gradual arousal with Marge O'Day, no caressing culmination of the senses brought to a fever pitch. It was all smotheringly, encompassingly there at once, from her deep groans to her pillowy breasts and when she finally shuddered heavily against him and clamped his face into her breasts he felt his own groan of utter satiation.

She lay beside him, the heavy breasts heaving as she drew in deep gasps of air. "Real good, big man," she murmured. "I overwhelm most men but not you."

"You give it a good try, honey," Fargo commented and she chuckled as she sat up.

"Better too much than too little." Marge grinned as she reached over to take hold of the nightdress and he pressed a hand into the very full, round but still firm buttocks. "I've got to get back and sleep. Driving a team is damn hard," she said.

He stood up, slapped her on the rump and she hurried away through the trees. He lay down again, drew a deep sigh and embraced sleep until the yellow spatters of sunlight came through the leaves over his head. He rose, dressed and strode to where the Ovaro was tethered near the stage. He'd finished washing from his canteen when the others woke and he pointed out a clump of red currants and gooseberries that would provide a tasty breakfast. He had the Ovaro saddled and ready to ride when he saw Mitchell streaking toward him from behind the stage, the boy's smooth face white and tight.

"Dammit, you come back here, Mitchell Blake," he heard Charity shout as she came around the rear of the coach, her haze-blue eyes dark with anger. Mitchell skidded to a halt beside him, seized hold of his arm with a fierce desperation.

"Charity says I can't ride with you anymore. She says I can't be with you at all," he blurted out and Fargo lifted his eyes to the slender figure striding toward him.

"You've got some reason for this?" he asked and Charity's haze-blue eyes held icy disdain.

"I certainly do," she snapped.

"I'd sure like to hear it," Fargo said.

"Me, too," Mitchell added angrily.

Charity cast an icy glare at the boy. "You mind your tongue, Mitchell Blake," she snapped. "And you go back to the stage and wait there. I'll discuss this with Fargo." Mitchell glared back and continued to hang on to Fargo's arm until Fargo put a hand atop the boy's head.

"Go on, do as you're told, Mitchell. I'll be along soon," he said reassuringly. Mitchell slowly released his hold on Fargo's arm and trudged away, hands clenched into small fists. Fargo turned to Charity as she glared at him.

"You see, he listens to you instead of me," she said.

"Is that what this is all about?" Fargo asked.

"No, this is about my responsibility for the boy's moral health. I don't want him looking up to you as an example of anything," Charity flung back.

"What's put a burr up your little ass?"

"My, you do have a way with words," Charity said with a sniff.

"When they fit," Fargo said.

Charity's voice lowered a notch but her haze-blue eyes were dark fire. "I saw Marge O'Day return last night," she said. "I was a fool. When you decided to help us I really thought it meant you had a conscience. I see now it only meant you had an arrangement to satisfy your sexual appetite."

"You're forgetting something, honey."

"Such as?"

"I could have both, a conscience and an appetite." He smiled cheerfully.

She paused for a moment. "Sorry, that's entirely too convenient for you," she snapped.

"And too upsetting for you," Fargo said. "You can't see a saint and a sinner in the same package. Hell, that'd mean you'd have to take another look at yourself."

"Nonsense."

Fargo's eyes turned ice-hard. "I'll tell you again, you're handling the boy wrong. A young horse needs some loose rein. So does a boy. You hold him in too tight and you're asking for trouble," he said.

"He's my responsibility. I'll handle him as I see fit," she said stiffly.

"He's on this stage. That makes him my responsibility, too. He sees me as a friend, someone to enjoy the trip with."

"He has to learn about picking the right kind of friends," Charity said.

"He doesn't need your tight-assed ideas about behavior. You're his governess, not a damn jailer,"

Fargo threw back at her. "I'm going to do you a favor and talk to him and you'd best listen to me, too."

"I don't need your help," Charity hissed.

"Hell you don't," Fargo tossed at her over his shoulder as he strode to the stage. He wrestled with words as he walked. The boy was her charge and he didn't want to destroy her authority. But he didn't want the kind of trouble she could bring on with her damfool attitude. He'd talk to the boy as a confidant, he decided. Mitchell would like that and could turn his resentment into patience. With a little touch of quiet conspiracy to help it along, Fargo grunted and saw Mitchell look up as he appeared at the stage. The boy wiped the glower from his face as Fargo halted beside him and leaned against the big rear wheel.

"Did you tell her not to bother me?" Mitchell asked.

Fargo let his lips purse. "Got us a little problem, Mitchell," he said. "I can't go telling Charity what to do. She's your governess. What's right is right. It's going to be up to you and me; for the moment, mostly you."

"What do you mean?" Mitchell frowned.

"You've got to give her some time to cool off," Fargo said. "She's really more mad at me than you."

"Why?" Mitchell asked and Fargo almost winced at the question.

"She's corralled a lot of damfool wrong ideas," Fargo said. "Neither of us can change that in a hurry. You know why I decided to come along and that's still strictly between us."

Mitchell nodded.

"You just go along with her for now, Mitchell, let her have her way until she simmers down. I'd guess by the end of the day she'll change her tune," Fargo said.

"If you say so, Fargo," Mitchell agreed. "But I know her. She's real strict."

"We'll see," Fargo said, pressed a hand into the boy's shoulder. "Now let's get with the others." He started away with Mitchell happily going along beside him and strode around to the other side of the stage. Charity, her face stiff, waited with the others and avoided his eyes. "We'll stay in the hills—move carefully," Fargo said. "I want Myrna on the roof along with you, Holman."

"On the roof?" Holman blurted.

"That's right. You'll just sit there, cross-legged," Fargo said. "The Crow will be watching us every damn minute. The more we can do to keep them wondering the better chance we have. If we can keep them uneasy about us, keep them off-balance, maybe we can just bluff our way through the heart of Crow country. Now let's move."

Fargo waited as Holman and Myrna climbed onto the roof of the roadcoach; then he swung onto the Ovaro. He paused beside Marge. "I'll be staying close for the most part," he told her.

"I'll like that." Marge chuckled and he kept his smile inside himself as he moved on. But he saw Pauline Beal's snapping blue eyes take on a tiny glint of quick interest. He led the stage on through a path between tall firs, down into a small mountain valley, paused to let the horses rest. As the day wore on, he seemed to be traveling aimlessly but he continued to move north, albeit circuitously. He rode at the front of the team, staying in place. But his eyes swept the higher land and watched the heavy tree cover. The signs were there, the motion of branches being brushed back in a straight line, little knots of activity disturbing thick brush in different places. The Crow were watching them, and staying back, Fargo nodded to himself. It was still working. They were still definitely uneasy about this stagecoach and its strange cargo of passengers.

But they also had no reason to rush anything. Fargo grunted with grimness. They could wait and attack when they were certain it was the right thing to do. He sent the Ovaro into a canter and took the horse up a narrow passageway that opened to his right as the stage rolled on below. It was his one venture away from the coach for the day and he halted at a high ridge where he could scan the land beyond. His eyes moved slowly across the terrain, paused and grew narrow. Something moved far back in the hills, very far back, but he had caught the faint smudge of dust that rose into the air. Another set of Crow, perhaps. Or some other passing tribe, he muttered silently. But maybe something else, someone following, he added as he turned the pinto and went down through the hills to where he caught up to the stage and resumed his place in front of the team.

Dusk began to gather and the Crow continued to do nothing but watch and wait. Every hour helped and every day was one more day alive, he reminded himself as he took the stage into a thick stand of Rocky Mountain maple where a cluster of chokeberry would furnish dessert for the night meal.

"God, my legs are stiff," Myrna said as he helped her down from the roof of the coach. Delwin Ferris came to take her arm and lead her away and Fargo found Marge beside him as he sat down to one side with a length of beef jerky.

"Don't expect company tonight. I'm exhausted," she said. "This mountain driving has to stop."

"Another few days, if we're lucky," Fargo said.

"Let's hope." Marge sighed and moved on. Fargo munched on the jerky as the night fell and saw Charity sitting behind the coach with Mitchell beside her. She took a tin plate back to her bags and paused when she saw Fargo rise and get his bedroll.

"Getting ready for another night of pleasure?" Acid disdain filled her every word.

"You asking or offering?" Fargo said and saw her eyes flare at once.

"Lout," she hissed as she spun away and he let his laugh follow her to the stage before he disappeared into the trees with his bedroll. He undressed quickly and put the Colt beside him. Habit and caution more than anything else. The Crow wouldn't attack by night and it was still too soon for anyone following to catch up to them. The night deepened and he slept soundly with only the familiar forest sounds penetrating his subconscious. The moon was far across the night sky when he snapped awake, the sound cutting through the night, Charity's voice calling out.

"Mitchell, damn you. Come back here," Fargo heard her shout as he sat up, cursed as he drew on clothes. He strapped his gunbelt on as he ran to the stage and saw Pauline and Holman sitting up. Pauline pointed into the balsams to the left of the stage and Fargo strode forward, heard Charity call out again and came upon her as she pushed through a thick clump of barberry shrubs.

"Shut up," Fargo barked. "You trying to wake every Crow in the mountains?" She wore only her petticoat and a hastily donned blouse with the bottom buttons still opened to reveal a flat, slender stomach as she turned to him.

"He's run away," she said.

"I figured that much. Why, dammit?" Fargo growled.

"Because he's a headstrong, disobedient child," Charity said.

"What'd you say to make him run?" Fargo pressed.

"Nothing," Charity said but he saw the mask slide over her haze-blue eyes.

"Bullshit," Fargo snapped. "He wouldn't just run off. What'd you say, dammit?"

She drew righteousness around her as though it were a cloak. "I told him he was going to stay away from you if I had to tie him up and I wasn't changing my mind about that," Charity answered. "It's my duty to do what I think is best for the boy."

"You're not doing what you think's best for him. You're frustrating him with your tight-assed attitudes. This is all your fault, dammit."

"It's just as much yours," Charity snapped.

"Mine?"

"Yes. He ran looking for you. If you'd been here instead of off indulging yourself he'd have found you," she said.

"I was indulging myself in sleep. How long has he been gone?"

Charity shrugged. "Maybe an hour. I woke and found him gone," she said.

"He's probably lost by now," Fargo said. "Come on back to the stage."

"Can't you look for him?" Charity asked. "We've got to find him."

"I'd never pick up tracks in these woods at night. Dawn's only an hour or so away. I'll look for him then," Fargo said and she hurried beside him back to the stage. The others were awake, waiting, and Ferris was the first to pose the question.

"What happened? Why'd the boy run away?" he asked, and Charity fastened him with a stiff glance.

"Because he's a stubborn, willful child," she said.

"He ran for the same reason a colt breaks away when you hold him in too tight," Fargo cut in and Charity's lips tightened as she glared at him.

"Think you can find him come morning?" Pauline asked.

Fargo shrugged grimly. "I hope so, but we're only a few miles from the main Crow camp. They could find him first," he said and saw Charity's eyes grow wide.

"You didn't tell me that," she said.

"I'm telling you now," he muttered.

"What happens if they find him first?" Marge broke in.

Fargo frowned in thought before answering. "They

93

don't know what to make of us yet. There's a good chance they'd hold him to see what happens," he said.

"See what happens?" Delwin Ferris repeated. "Just what does that mean?"

"We'll go into that tomorrow if we have to," Fargo said.

"I'd like that explained now," Ferris snapped.

Fargo speared the man with eyes that had suddenly become ice-floe cold. "Tomorrow," he growled.

Ferris swallowed and turned away and Fargo waited till the others had all settled back into their places before he slid down against a wide-trunked fir. He silently swore at Charity once more, closed his eyes and slept, unwilling to think about tomorrow.

5

He was on his feet as the first pink-gray streaks of dawn touched the forest. He saw Charity start to come from inside the stage as he started for the heavy tree cover. "Stay here with the others," he rasped. He saw her halt and he hurried to the edge of the trees, his eyes sweeping the ground. He found the single set of small footprints after a few minutes. Mitchell had circled the area of the stage, he saw, and finally gone straight west. Fargo crouched low as he strained to pick up the small prints the forest carpet had already begun to swallow up. But Mitchell had run hard, aimlessly but desperately, and he'd dug heels hard into the ground. The prints stayed clear enough despite the speed with which the grass sprang back with the dawn dew.

They also stayed almost straight west, Fargo noted and swore under his breath. The new day came in to send the sun into the woods and Fargo broke into a long, loping run as he followed Mitchell's prints. He saw the slope in front of him, followed it up and halted to peer down the other side where he could see the Crow camp in the distance with the river coursing beside it. The small footprints headed straight toward the camp and Fargo stayed in his crouch as he went forward. Running through the night with only the last of the moonlight above, Mitchell couldn't have seen the Crow camp until he was almost atop it, Fargo frowned as he slowed, dropped to one knee where he could see the camp clearly.

Slowly, he scanned the length of the camp as squaws emerged from tipis and sleeping forms on the ground woke, rose to become Crow warriors. "Goddamn," Fargo muttered in a whisper as he scanned the edge of the camp along the river and found the stake driven into the ground, the small form tied to it, arms pulled back around the stake.

It took little imagination to know what happened. Mitchell had blundered into the camp, or certainly to the edge of it where he'd been seized. Fargo's eyes were narrowed in grim thought as he watched the Crow move past the boy, some pause to frown at him, others quickly give the tied figure a wide berth. He waited and the chief with the prominent nose and eagle feather in his headband emerged from his tipi. Accompanied by three braves, he went to Mitchell, halted a dozen paces from the boy and stared at the small, bound figure.

A fourth figure came to stand beside the chief and Fargo saw a shaman's medicine bundle in the man's hand. He and the chief stared at the boy for a few minutes more, exchanged half-whispered words and both slowly turned away and disappeared into the tipi. The other three braves waited a few minutes longer but they also turned away finally. Fargo stayed motionless as he scanned the camp again, his eyes moving along the river to where Mitchell was tied to the stake. The boy was awake and Fargo saw as much defiance in his small, unlined face as fear. Silently, Fargo moved backward, retreated a dozen yards farther and then turned and moved away in the long, loping crouch. Thoughts raced through his mind as he ran, none of them good. Only one fact offered any hope at all. The Crow had reacted as he'd hoped they would and that left a slim chance, Fargo murmured, a damn slim one.

The others turned to him as one when he reached the stage, Myrna with a piece of johnnycake in one hand. "You didn't find him," Charity said with dismay in her voice.

"Nothing that good. I found him," Fargo said. "He wandered into the Crow camp."

"Oh, my God," Charity breathed and fell back against the front wheel of the stage.

"What have they done with him?" Pauline asked.

"Nothing yet. They're waiting," Fargo said.

"To see what happens?" Ferris frowned, irritation in his voice, and Fargo nodded. "Maybe you'd like to explain that now," the man snapped.

"They're still uneasy about us. If we try to save him or if we take off, they'll know he's nothing special and we're not, either. They'll come down on us fast and hard," Fargo said. "They're in the high hills watching us right now, I guarantee you."

"And Mitchell?" Charity asked.

"He's tied to a stake. They'll keep him there till tomorrow morning. If he's freed by the Great Spirit it'll mean he's special, not to be touched. The same for us," Fargo said.

"Hell, of course he's not going to be freed by any Great Spirit," Holman said. "That leaves us no-place."

"It leaves me tonight to get him free without any sign that we did it."

"That's impossible." Ferris frowned. "Absolutely impossible."

"Maybe, but I'm going to try."

"Ridiculous. It can't be done. I say we wait till dark and pull out, get away from here by the time morning comes," Ferris said.

"And just leave Mitchell?" Charity cut in. "What kind of monster are you?"

"It seems you caused the boy to run," Ferris shot back. "I'm sorry but I can't see that we all should die because of one willful boy."

"I can't see leaving the boy," Pauline said.

"He can't be freed without their knowing we did it," Ferris said.

"I'm going to try, I told you," Fargo said. "You better pray it can be done because it's your only ticket out of here in one piece."

He turned away from the others but Pauline came up to him, her snapping blue eyes probing into him. "You don't have the first notion of how you're going to do this, do you?" she slid at him.

"Not yet," Fargo admitted. "But I've all day to think about it. Might even sleep on it."

Pauline laughed and the skin at the corners of her eyes crinkled more than usual. "You're some-thing special, Fargo, and I've seen a lot in my years," she said as she strode away. Fargo had started for the trees when Cyrus Holman called to him.

"We just going to sit around all day?" the man asked.

"That's right," Fargo said. "Catch up on your sleep, relax, think. But be quiet, as if nothing's happened." Fargo walked on and slid down against a tree, closed his eyes and let his mind and his body relax. He half-slept in the warmth of the day, let his mind become a blank sheet against which plans and thoughts slowly outlined themselves, slid along on their own, jostled each other, vied for attention. He drifted into a complete sleep only to wake and let his mind parade thoughts again, re-examined each, discarded, retained, reviewed and the day wore on with painful slowness. The others remained quiet but he could feel the tensions of fear and anger that rolled out in silent, invisible waves.

The dusk finally came and he knew the Crow were moving down from the high hills, breaking off their watch. But he remained against the tree and gave them more than enough time to return to their camp before he rose with the last of the dusk still clinging, a purple gauze over the hills. He walked to the stage and saw the others rise to face him.

"Give me a hand," he said to Holman as he put his shoulder to the door of the stage. Holman stepped forward, added his arms and Fargo lifted the door up and out of its hinges and put it down against the coach.

"What in the hell are you going to do with that?" Ferris pushed at him.

"They have Mitchell on a stake only a few feet from the river beside the camp. I need something flat to get him away without leaving footprints in the softness of the river bank," Fargo explained. "The door's far from perfect but it'll have to do." He turned to Charity, his jaw set tight. "I'm going to need an extra pair of hands."

"Of course," she said. "I insist."

"Good, because you're going whether you want to or not," he said.

"Can't you ever be gracious about anything?"

"There are times. This isn't one of them," Fargo said. "Unhitch one of the horses."

"I'll give you a hand," Pauline said as Charity strode to the team and began to unhitch the right lead horse.

"Leave the lead and bridle on," Fargo ordered as he swung onto the Ovaro. "You ride him. I'll carry the door with me." He turned to the others. "You wait here. Stay quiet," he said and pulled the door of the stage up alongside him as he sent the Ovaro forward. Charity followed close at his heels, then came up alongside him as he rode up the first long slope.

"What if you can't pull it off right? We can still take Mitchell and run, can't we?" she asked.

"None of us will run very far," Fargo answered harshly as he sent the Ovaro over the top of the slope and down the other side. He turned south when he saw the river outlined under the almost full moon. He made a wide circle and reached the river downwind of the Crow camp, reined up and slid from the saddle. He put the door of the coach on the ground, tethered Charity's mount to the same branch he tied the Ovaro to as she swung from the horse. He pushed into a big hackberry and broke off a long length of branch with a thick bundle of leaves at one end. Putting the branch atop the door he began to pull off clothes.

"What are you doing?" Charity asked, instant alarm in her voice.

"We're going to swim upriver to the camp. It's the only way we can get close to Mitchell. Get your clothes off," he said.

"I'll do nothing of the sort."

He paused as he started to take off his jeans. "You going to do it or am I?" he asked.

"You would do such a thing, wouldn't you?" Charity accused.

"You can count on it," Fargo said.

"I can swim in my clothes," she said.

"Not tonight you can't. Wet white man's clothing will smell. Some half-asleep brave is likely to pick it up and we're finished," he told her as he finished stripping off the jeans. He saw Charity's haze-blue eyes move over the powerful beauty of his body before she spun away.

"I won't have Mitchell see me naked," she said.

"Mitchell will be too exhausted, too scared and too busy to notice whether you're wearing a ball gown," Fargo said. "Get undressed, dammit. Time's wasting."

She stayed with her back to him, stiff as a ramrod, but he saw her begin to open buttons. The dress fell to her feet, then the petticoat and finally long, pink bloomers and he saw a beautifully curved, slender but strong back with a narrow waist, long legs that were lovely and a firm rear as tight and small as it had seemed under her dresses. She took three quick steps into the river and sank into the water to her chin before she turned to glare at him. He took the long branch to the water and reached out to her with it. "Swim with this out of the water. Hold it over your head. I want the leaves dry. That's important, understand?" he said. She nodded and he felt her eyes on him as he stepped into the river with the door of the coach. Pushing the door ahead of him through the water, he began to swim slowly upriver.

It would take time before they reached the Crow camp but that was all to the good. They'd all be hard asleep by then and he cast a glance up at the almost full moon and swore under his breath. Charity swam beside him, holding the branch high, transferring it from arm to arm as she used long, slow strokes. She made certain she swam with only arms and head above water. They finally reached a slow bend in the small river and he motioned to Charity as he slowed and began to almost drift around the bend. The Crow camp came into sight at once, dark and sleeping, a small fire burning in the center of the tipi area.

His gaze went to the shore and he spotted the stake and the small figure tied to it. Mitchell's head was hanging in exhaustion, he saw. "No sentries?" Charity whispered at his elbow as she treaded water.

"Sentries would insult the Great Spirit," Fargo whispered back. "They don't want to do that if he comes for Mitchell. If he doesn't come they're confident Mitchell will be right there come dawn."

He pushed forward slowly, shifted directions with the coach door and reached the edge of the bank directly in front of the stake. He stayed in the water, waited and saw Mitchell raise his head. The boy's tired eyes stared out and slowly began to widen as he focused on the figure crouched in the water in front of him. Fargo held a finger to his lips and Mitchell, his mouth open in shock and joy, continued to stare. Slowly, Fargo lifted the stage door out of the water, crept another six inches up the bank but continued to stay in the water. He reached forward, using all the strength of his arm and shoulder muscles to keep the heavy door held flat out, and lowered the door onto the bank.

He rested a moment, drew in deep breaths and glanced at Charity who still held the branch in the air. "You stay right here," he breathed and stood up. Reaching out with one leg, he stepped on the door of the coach, brought the other foot up onto the other edge. Moving carefully, distributing his balance evenly across the door, he lowered himself to his knees at the top end of the door where he was only a foot from Mitchell. Slowly he turned onto his back, lay on the door and reached up and back to find the knots that bound the boy's wrists. The rawhide thongs made a tight knot and he worked carefully. They couldn't be cut or the entire charade would be exposed and he had to halt often to rest his fingers. Finally, he loosened one knot enough, worked further on it and it came apart. The other one continued to resist but he stayed with it, felt the little beads of perspiration rolling down his face. They had tied an intricate, Crow knot of intertwining strands and he saw the moon above moving down the far edge of the sky and he hurried his efforts. He almost let out a gasp of glee as he finally felt the main strand of rawhide give, pull away and the others come apart.

Mitchell brought his arms around at once and rubbed circulation back into his wrists as Fargo sat up. He held a finger to his lips again, gestured to the door as he rose to his knee and held one hand out to Mitchell. The boy took his hand, wavered but managed to get one foot on the door and pull the other leg behind him. He nodded understanding as Fargo motioned for him to walk across the coach door and into the water. When Mitchell sank into the river, Fargo slid down across the door and slid backward until he felt the cool water close around his feet and ankles. He halted when he was half into the river, lifted the door up and pulled it the rest of the way with him and lowered it into the water without making a ripple. He motioned to Charity and she handed the branch to him and he went to the bank again, reached out with the dry leaves of the branch and drew them back and forth across the soft ground of the bank until all traces of the door were gone.

He paused and surveyed the scene. The riverbank was unmarked, the stake standing alone and the rawhide thongs untied and uncut lay on the ground beside it. He grunted in satisfaction, turned in the water and took hold of the door again and pushed it in front of him as he began to swim downriver. He let Charity and Mitchell go ahead of him as he swept the Crow camp. Nothing moved, the camp still hard asleep and he swam on slowly and silently. Charity had one arm around Mitchell, he saw, helping the small, exhausted form, and when they finally reached the spot where they'd left the horses, he stepped from the water first, lifted Mitchell up in his arm and carried him to the Ovaro.

Mitchell's small form clung to him, arms around his neck as he put the boy on the saddle. "It's all over. You can sleep on the way back," Fargo murmured and Mitchell nodded as he clung. Fargo glanced at Charity and smiled. She had flown into her clothes, not pausing to dry herself at all, and she hurried toward him. "Take the Ovaro with Mitchell," he said and she pulled herself into the saddle. He gathered his clothes, laid them across the withers of the team horse and swung onto the animal to ride naked behind Charity, the stage door at his side. The night wind had dried his body by the time they reached the forest of balsams and he halted to pull on clothes while Charity waited and watched.

"I'm really grateful to you," she said as, dressed, he came up alongside her. "You're a strange man, full of contradictions."

"Maybe," he allowed as they came in sight of the coach. The figures hurried out of the stage and rushed forward and he saw Pauline Beal's eyes focus on Charity and Mitchell.

"By God, you did it," she gasped, reached up and lifted Mitchell down from the horse. "By God," she repeated in awe.

"This means we're all safe now," Ferris said.

"You've a one-track mind," Fargo said to the man. "But the answer is yes. They'll find Mitchell gone and no sign of anyone having set him free. They'll be convinced the Great Spirit is protecting him." He cast a glance up at the still-black sky as he dismounted. "Now, I'm going to get me a few hours' sleep and I don't aim to be disturbed," he said and strode into the trees with his bedroll. He had his eyes closed before he finished stretching out and he slept heavily to wake only when the sun touched his face through the thick foliage overhead.

He rose, shook away the vestiges of sleep and dressed. Mitchell was first to spot him as he reached the stage and the boy raced to him, threw his arms around the tall, sturdy legs. "I knew you'd come for me, Fargo. I knew you'd find a way," the boy murmured. Fargo held him for a moment and then pulled him back.

"No more running away," he said severely. "No more getting so mad you don't think straight."

"No more," Mitchell said.

"Charity came with me, remember," Fargo said. "She risked her neck for you."

"I know," Mitchell said and looked very adult. "We had a long talk. She said I could be with you whenever you'd let me."

"Good enough. For now you ride in the stage with her," Fargo said and Mitchell nodded happily, stood by and watched as Fargo put the door back onto the coach. The others boarded and Marge took the reins, her eyes on Fargo as he brought the pinto alongside.

"You and Miss Prim and Proper all made up?" Marge slid at him.

"She came through. I give her credit for that," he said and was surprised at the acid tolerance in Marge's smile. He shook his head inwardly and sent the pinto on, rode forward slowly as the stage rolled after him. He scanned the high hills. Nothing moved save a flight of ruffed grouse. The Crow had their answer and it would be enough. They'd stay away, unwilling to anger the Great Spirit.

Fargo spotted a level pathway between hills and led the stage onto it as he rode ahead. He halted when the morning grew late and let the horses rest and rode on again. He'd gone perhaps a few hundred yards when he yanked the Ovaro to a halt.

He felt the frown dig into his brow as he stared ahead at the line of bronzed figures that blocked the passage. In the center of the line the Crow chief with the eagle feather stared back at him. Fargo was still peering at the silent, motionless figures when the stage rolled to a halt beside him. Delwin Ferris, his face darkened with anger, pushed his head out of the stage window. "What's this mean?" he hissed.

"I don't know. They're not supposed to be here," Fargo said.

"Not supposed to be here? Dammit, you lied to us. They know. That's why they're here. You didn't pull it off," Ferris rasped.

"Shut up," Fargo barked. "Maybe there's another reason," he added with more confidence than he felt. He saw Charity step from the coach, Mitchell's frightened face behind her as Fargo swung from the Ovaro and walked forward. The Crow chief leaped from his pony with a smooth, quick motion, his right fist clenched. He halted, opened his hand and tossed an object at Fargo's feet and the Trailsman stared down at the gold bracelet. He kept his face expressionless as he lifted his eyes to the Indian.

"On the bank where the boy was tied," the Crow said in Siouan. Fargo flicked a glance at Charity, saw her blink and silently cursed. His face impassive, he returned his eyes to the chief.

"Why bring this to me?" he asked.

"White squaw bracelet."

"The river brought it," Fargo said.

"No," the Crow chief answered.

"Yes," Fargo said firmly. "The Great Spirit set the boy free."

"Bracelet says no," the Indian insisted and Fargo's eyes narrowed as his thoughts raced. The Crow chief had come, accused, and that meant he was not certain. If he were certain he'd have simply attacked. He would have to be met in his own way.

"You make big talk," Fargo said to the chief. "You cannot swear your words on the sacred medicine bundle," he said and saw the flicker in the Indian's black eyes and he knew he had struck at the core of it.

"There must be another sign," the Crow said, yanked a tomahawk from his waist and sent it plunging into the ground. The gesture needed no more words.

"What's going on?" he heard Holman call.

"They want more proof that the Great Spirit is

protecting us," Fargo said. "They want the sign of combat. The winner will show who the Great Spirit is protecting." The Crow chief raised his arm and pointed to the others beside the stage. "Choose," he demanded in Siouan and no translation was needed. Fargo tossed a quick glance at Holman and Ferris. "Any volunteers?" he asked with a wry snort he let escape his lips. The Indian waited and Fargo tapped himself on the chest. The Crow took a bone hunting knife from the waistband of his loincloth and tossed it to the ground. Fargo unstrapped his gunbelt and dropped it beside him.

"What are you doing? Shoot him!" Holman rasped.

"I do that and you're all dead in three seconds," Fargo said. "The combat has to be bare-handed, no weapons to give an advantage to either according to the Crow ways." He stepped forward and the line of horsemen moved their mounts back to allow more room for the battle. Fargo took in the chief again as the man came toward him. He was well-built, not an ounce of fat on him, all long, sinewy muscle. He would kick, bite, gouge and do whatever else he could to win. He'd fight as the wolverine fights, using every part of his body to kill his foe and Fargo felt the grimness settle over him as the Indian began to circle him. Fargo moved in a counter-circle and let the Indian come in closer, staying on the balls of his feet, and his eyes, fixed on the man's shoulders, caught the tiny ripple of muscles contracting as the Indian swung, leaped forward and swung again.

Fargo pulled away, twisted, and the Indian went past him to spin around and face him again. Fargo backed, let the Crow come at him again and he was ready when the bronzed form lunged forward, long arms outstretched. He ducked low, brought up a looping left that caught the Crow flush on the jaw. The Indian went down as he flew backward. Most men would have stayed down but the Crow rose at once. The rage to kill and to win gave him power of a special kind and this time he came forward more carefully. Fargo waited, circled to the left, feinted with a left and sent a right cross whistling through the air. But the Crow was quick, ducking away as the blow grazed his jaw. He shot out one leg, hooked a moccasined foot behind Fargo's ankle and pulled. Fargo felt himself go off balance. He half-fell sideways, tried to recover but the Crow was onto him with the quick fury of a puma. Fargo felt the man's hands close around his throat, steel fingers digging in, and breath came hard almost at once.

He let himself go down backward, let his weight pull the Indian with him but the man's hands did not leave his throat. Fargo brought up one leg, pushed his knee into the Crow's belly and used all the strength of his thigh muscles to drive it upward. He heard the Indian grunt in pain and the hands on his throat came loose only for a moment but the moment was all he needed. He drove a short right up into the Crow's abdomen and the Indian fell away. Fargo rolled, tried to smash a blow down onto the Crow's face but the man twisted his head aside and rolled away. He was on his feet in one quick bound as Fargo came up swinging and the Crow ducked back, avoided the long, looping blow.

Fargo drew back, crouched, watched the black fury in the Indian's eyes as the man came at him with short, darting movements, feinting with his body and shoulders. Fargo tried a long left hook, saw the Indian's foot come out to curl behind his leg again but he was ready for it and pulled away. Suddenly the Crow leaped straight up into the air, spun, came down on both feet, leaped up again, spun and came down but this time as he came down he lunged forward without a break in his movements. Fargo cursed as he tried to twist away and felt the Indian slam into him and realized the explosion of leaps and spins had accomplished their objective, to freeze him in surprise and astonishment for a precious split second. The chief's head hit into his stomach and Fargo felt the air push out of him as he went down on his back. He twisted his head to one side as he saw the Indian's fingers come down to gouge at his eyes, cursed and felt the surge of desperate fury race through his body. With a roar, he twisted, slammed both fists into the Indian's ribs and the bronze, sinewy form slid half-off him. Half-off was enough and Fargo circled the Indian's neck with one arm, closed hard and spun and the man half-catapulted over him.

The Crow hit the ground facedown and Fargo opened his arm, drew it back as the Indian started to roll. He moved with the near-naked form, brought his fist down in a hammerlike blow that smashed into the Crow's face. The Indian cried out in pain as his nose smashed into bits and red gushed from his flattened nostrils. But he lunged forward again, fingers outstretched to ram into his foe's eyes. Fargo ducked low, twisted, let his shoulder meet the charge and the Crow hit, bounced backward. Fargo's driving left followed, hit the Crow's jaw and the Indian went down. Fargo dived atop him and, too late, saw the Crow kick out straight with both feet. The blow caught Fargo full in the abdomen and he felt the wind go from him as he grunted in pain and fell backward. The Crow rolled to his feet, dived, and Fargo managed to get one arm up in a backward swing as he fought to regain his breath. His forearm caught the Crow against the side of the face as he came in, with enough force to deflect the lunge and send the Indian past him. Fargo spun, saw the Crow dive for his leg and kicked out. The blow only caught the Indian on the shoulder but it was enough to send him off balance and he hit the ground on his side.

Fargo aimed another kick but the Crow was quick as a cat, rolled away, got both his hands around the big man's ankle and yanked and Fargo went down hard on his back. He brought one knee up as the Indian dived at him, smashed it into the man's chest and the Crow fell away. But he spun, his lips drawn back and Fargo saw him lunge forward to sink his teeth into flesh and bone. Fargo flung himself to the left, heard the Crow's teeth snap together as they grazed the muscles of his neck. He whirled, on one knee, let the Crow dive at him again. He measured distances, swung a looping left hook that crashed into the Indian's jaw. The sinewy, raging figure straightened up, staggered, and Fargo's right cross came in with the power of a piledriver. The Crow took the blow full on the jaw, staggered again and went down on his side. He started to roll and Fargo stepped in, bringing his fist down in a tremendous sledgehammer blow, every ounce of his strength behind it.

The gargantuan blow crashed down onto the Crow's throat and Fargo felt and heard the crunching, crackling sound of the small larynx bones as they shattered. The Indian rolled onto his side, hoarse, rattling sounds squeezed from his throat as the blood began to spit from his lips. He pulled himself onto his hands and knees, head hanging down, tried to rise to his feet even as the blood became a small gusher that poured out of his mouth. Fargo brought his arm up again, as much in mercy as anger this time, smashed one more hammerlike blow down, this time on the back of the man's neck. The Crow dropped facedown on the ground, breathed a last, rattled gasp and lay still.

Fargo straightened up, drew a long breath and looked up at the line of bronze-skinned figures. Two slipped from their mounts, walked to the lifeless form and lifted the chief from the ground. He left a trail of red spilling onto the soil as they laid him across the back of his pony. Silently, not looking back, the Crow rode slowly away to disappear into the thick forest. Fargo drew in another deep breath and turned to where the others waited beside the stage. His face a rigid mask, he halted in front of Charity. "The goddamn bracelet, you knew about it, didn't you?" he said through lips that hardly moved.

"It slipped off my wrist when we started to leave," she murmured.

"Why didn't you tell me?" Fargo exploded with a roar, and Charity flinched.

"I expected it'd go to the bottom. I didn't think the current would wash it ashore," she said.

"You're real good at not thinking," Fargo bit out. "Get in the stage," he said with disgust and anger, including the others in his harsh glance. He climbed onto the Ovaro and felt the pull of shoulder muscles still strained. He rode slowly, left the stage when the day wore down and climbed a slope to a place in the high hills that let him sweep the land behind with a long, careful survey. He picked up the sign in a few minutes, the motion of distant trees, the faint thickness of the air that followed the movement of the tree branches. They were being followed, he grunted as his lips grew tight. No Crow, this time. Men riding hard through the forests, following exactly in the tracks left by the stage. He watched the trees sway as the riders dipped into the narrow ravine where he'd taken the stage only twenty-four hours earlier.

He swore and turned the pinto down the slope, rode on and came onto the narrow road below as the stage appeared. He came alongside and motioned Marge to halt. "We've an hour or so of daylight left. I'll find us a spot to camp and we'll talk some," he said.

"About what?" Holman frowned out of the window.

"About why we're still being followed," Fargo said and beckoned to Mitchell. "Let's ride some, son," he called and Mitchell tore out of the stage and onto the Ovaro. Fargo cantered on and cast an eye

114

at the sky that had already begun to hint at more than dusk. "We're going to have a storm, Mitchell, heavy rain, I'd guess," Fargo said.

"How do you know?" Mitchell asked and Fargo pointed to a flock of slate-colored juncos winging across the sky.

"The birds are flying low," he said. "And look at the trees. The leaves are showing their backs." Mitchell nodded and settled against him as they rode.

"Charity's real sorry about that bracelet," Mitchell said.

"She tell you to tell me that?" Fargo questioned.

"No. She'd be mad if I told you. But I know her," Mitchell said. "She's been real quiet. She's always like that when she's upset."

"She ought to be upset," Fargo growled as he rode on and dusk drifted down from the high hills. He reined to a halt at the foot of a steep and narrow trail that appeared, heavy tree cover on one side and a sheer drop into a ravine on the other. He dismounted and peered up along the trail. It ran steep and straight up into the high hills, wide enough to take the stage but with little room to spare and his brow furrowed as he turned away. A half-circle of hawthorns a dozen yards from the steep passage offered a good resting place for the night as they formed an arched roof. Fargo held the Ovaro still as Mitchell slid to the ground and he waved the stage into the hawthorns when it rolled up. He tethered the Ovaro to one side as the others climbed from the coach, their eyes on the Trailsman as he faced them. "Who's first?" he barked.

"Nobody's first," Delwin Ferris answered, letting indignation touch his voice. "Nobody knows why we're being followed."

"Bullshit," Fargo said. "I just want to give you one more chance at telling the truth."

"I daresay those following us have nothing to do with the original attack," Ferris insisted.

"And the cow jumped over the moon," Fargo snorted. "Get some sleep. It's not going to get any easier." He turned away, took his bedroll and headed for the trees beyond the half-circle when Marge stepped in front of him, her lips pursed as she studied his tight face.

"Why is it so important?" she asked and he frowned at her. "To find out who's lying," she added.

"I like to know why I'm being shot at," Fargo said.

"What if you find out? You going to throw whoever it is off the stage?" she pressed.

He thought for a moment. "I might, if it'd mean saving everyone else," he answered. "And maybe if I knew the truth I could make it work for all of us. I haven't decided on that, yet. The point is, I'm going to find out."

She shrugged. "Seems to me it doesn't make any difference, now. We're being followed. I don't care why."

He let his eyes probe into her. "I do. You worried about what I might find out, Marge?" he asked and saw her eyes darken.

"Curious, that's all," she snapped. "And that remark just took care of any idea I had about paying you a visit tonight."

"Kind of touchy, aren't we," Fargo commented as she strode past him. He watched as she went into the stage and the frown stayed with him while he walked into the woods. The exchange had left an unpleasant taste in his mouth. He had hoped Marge was out of it, he realized, but her questioning had been more than curiosity. She was apprehensive, despite her protestations to the contrary. Damn, he swore silently as he set down his bedroll, undressed and stretched out. He drew sleep around himself at once and slept heavily until the first raindrops woke him. He sat up in the darkness, pulled on clothes and crept back to where he'd left the Ovaro. He pulled on his rain slicker, slid down against a tree and returned to sleep as the rain began to pour down in a heavy, unceasing deluge.

He watched the gray dawn come when he woke again and the others began to rummage for raingear. Some had weather clothes, others made do with sheets. Pauline Beal just let herself be drenched and saw him watching her. "I'll save my dry clothes inside my bag," she said. Mitchell, in a yellow rain slicker, ran over to him.

"You were right, Fargo," he said. "It's sure raining."

"It's going to get worse," Fargo said. "You make sure you do exactly what I tell you to do later. Charity, too."

"Yes, sir." Mitchell nodded gravely and hurried back to the stage.

"Get ready to roll," Fargo called out and saw Marge halt to stare at him.

"In this weather?" he frowned.

"Here and now," he snapped. Her eyes narrowed but she pulled a rain hat down harder over her head and started to climb up. Pauline followed her and he swept the others as they paused, saw the command in his eyes and boarded the coach. He swung onto the Ovaro and came alongside Marge. "We're going up that passage," he said.

Marge stared up at the narrow trail with the sheer drop at one edge. "You're crazy," she gasped.

"Drive slow and steady. Stay against the wall," he said and sent the Ovaro forward, waited, watched her bring the stagecoach to the bottom of the passageway and start the climb upward. The wheels of the roadcoach just fit onto the wide ledge and he watched the rain splash against the wheel rims as it coursed down the steep grade. He swung the Ovaro in behind the coach as the rain grew heavier, becoming a gray, wet curtain. Marge drove slowly, hugged the rock and shrub-lined side of the passage and let protruding branches brush against the roof and sides of the coach. Fargo wiped water from his eyes with increasing frequency as the downpour became a steady, driving deluge. He felt the earth under the Ovaro's hoofs begin to grow soft and he watched the wheels of the coach sink deeper into the ground. But they were still rolling well, only loosened dirt clinging to the rims, and he let the wagon go on. He guessed they were perhaps halfway up the passage when the water began to race downward with increasing force and depth, the ground no longer able to absorb any more of the rain. He heard the water splash against the Ovaro's ankles, and the wheels of the stage were now dripping mud with every turn.

Heavy rain continued to come down, smashing against his face with fury every time he raised his eyes to peer ahead and the racing water hissed as it ran down the passage. The horse's hoofs made a sucking sound with each step and Fargo squinted as he lifted his head to the sky. Only unbroken gray met his eyes through the pounding rain and he lowered his face, raising his voice in a shout that he knew would barely reach Marge. "Rein up," he called. "Rein up." He waited, watched the wheels roll to a halt and brought the Ovaro forward, slid from the horse and tied the reins to the back of the coach. He squeezed his way between the rock and brush and the side of the coach, slipped in the mud, landed on one knee and pulled himself up against the front wheel. "Everybody out," he called and sloshed forward to where Marge and Pauline sat on the open driver's seat. "That means you, too," he said and reached out and gave Pauline a helping hand down.

The others edged between the rock wall and the wheels of the stage to come forward. "The ground is starting to slide. The horses will never make it with a loaded stage," Fargo said. "You're all going to wait here while I take the stage the rest of the way up."

"We'll be soaked to the skin just waiting here," Myrna protested. "Why can't we go along behind?"

"If the horses lose footing and the coach starts to slide backward you'll be in big trouble," Fargo said. "I don't want to have to think about that. You wait here. You can't get much wetter, anyway." He turned away from the protest that stayed in their faces and took hold of the cheekstrap of the right lead horse, pulled gently and the horse began to move forward. The others came at once, digging hoofs into the soft ground that was now more mud than soil. He led the team very slowly, letting the horses feel their own way, exerting only the gentlest of pressure. He kept his head bent low as the rain continued to drive down with relentlessness. The storm was heavier than he'd expected, the rain coming down in gray sheets and he felt the rushing water sweep down the narrow passageway, slam into his ankles, bubble up and rush on its way again.

He didn't concern himself with the Ovaro tied to the back of the coach. If the team horses could make it, his surefooted pinto would have no trouble and he glanced down at the hoofs of the two lead horses. The rushing water prevented soft mud from clinging to their hoofs and he was grateful for that much but he could feel the horse beginning to slip. He swore into the steady rain. If the ground really began to slide the horses would quickly lose footing altogether. He dug one foot hard into the mud and cursed again as he failed to strike any firm layer of earth. The weight of the combined horses and coach was an advantage while the ground was merely rain-soaked, allowing better traction than a light rig would have. But the weight turned into a liability when the ground became sliding mud and it was perilously close to that, he realized.

He squinted up along the passage and again the

curtain of rain let him see only a few yards ahead. A small rock came down to hit against his leg, quickly followed by another. The topsoil was beginning to slide and he fought down the urge to hurry, forced himself to plod slowly ahead with one hand still clinging to the horse's cheekstrap. His foot slid out from under him and he went down, regained his feet and felt the ground suddenly begin to level off. He lifted his head, peered through the gray curtain of driving rain and glimpsed the top of the passage. A rock overhang on both sides marked the spot and he pulled himself forward, shook the rain from his eyes, and the rock overhang took shape, became a kind of high hill tunnel with heavy brush growth atop it.

The few minutes more it took to reach the top seemed an hour but he finally half-staggered under the rock overhang and the pelting rain vanished. He pulled the stage deeper into the tunnel of rock, untied the Ovaro, and the horse immediately shook itself. The team horses blew air, snorted and settled down, grateful to be standing still. Fargo took his lariat from the Ovaro, attached it to his belt under his raingear and stepped from the rock overhang. The rain pelted into him with what seemed instant glee and he began to move down the passage. He felt the ground slide from under him at once. He halted and began to inch his way down with little, careful steps. He moved steadily but slowly until he suddenly realized the driving downpour had lessened, the rain hitting at him with sprinkled gusts. But the treachery underfoot remained the same and he tested each step as the mud-covered soil moved under him.

When he finally spied the huddle of figures against the wall, the rain had halted but he continued to move slowly. Delwin Ferris shouted words when he reached the rain-soaked figures. "Damn you, Fargo, we're about drowned," the man said. "I'd have gone on but the boy put up such a damn fuss about staying."

"I agreed with Mitchell," Pauline put in and Fargo saw Charity nod and Marge shrug. Holman simply looked miserable.

"Good boy," Fargo said and the small figure in the yellow rain slicker beamed a smile back. Low, gray clouds scudded overhead, Fargo saw, signaling the end of the heavy rains. But the passage was a waiting mud slide, water still coursing down it from the rocks at one side. "You'll start up, in groups of two," Fargo said. "Stay ten yards apart. Slow, each step slow." He let his eyes move over the figures. "Charity and Mitchell, first," he said.

"Myrna and I are going first. I've indulged you in this long enough, dammit," Delwin Ferris snapped, pushed away from the wall and took Myrna with him. "And I'm not going to spend all damn day getting to a dry place," the man flung back.

"Slow, you damfool, slow," Fargo called as Ferris began to climb, slipping, digging in, slipping again but angrily pulling himself on. Fargo saw Myrna slip, go down and Ferris yank her up as he pushed forward. He shifted closer to the outside edge to find firmer ground. Fargo's lips thinned and he started after the man just as Ferris, taking a long forward stride, went down on all fours. Fargo saw the mud slide with him, his hand reach out to grab Myrna and miss as she went down on one knee.

"No, oh, Jesus," Ferris screamed as the mud slid out from under him, carrying him over the edge with his arms flailing. He disappeared.

Fargo dropped to his hands and knees, pushed his way along the mud until he was near enough to the edge to peer down. Ferris hung by his fingertips to an outcrop of rock, below him a straight drop to death. "Can't hold on," the man cried out. "Help me."

Fargo reached under his raingear, whipped the lariat out and rose to one knee. He leaned over as far as he dared before dropping the rope in a loop just wide enough to go over the clinging figure. He pulled it tight, felt the lariat catch around Ferris's waist and he dug one heel as deep into the mud as he could until he found the layer of soil still firm and dry enough to let him get a grip. He began to pull on the lariat and felt Ferris's body slowly lift. Twisting the rope around his arms, he continued to pull until Ferris's head appeared above the edge of the passage, his face drained of color.

Fargo halted, stared at the man. "More," Ferris said. "Get me up. Don't stop now."

"I want to know what you're running from," Fargo said. "I want the real reason why you're so damn desperate to get to Snow Bow."

"Are you mad? Not now. Not here."

"The truth," Fargo said. "Or I'm going to lose my grip on this lariat."

"All right, all right, but pull me up, first," the man gasped. "Jesus, pull me up."

"You get cute and I'll throw you back over," Fargo warned as he pulled on the rope. He reached out, grabbed Ferris by the arm and pulled him to safety. Ferris lay facedown in the muddy soil as he drew in deep gasps of air and finally he pushed himself up and stared at the big man still holding the lariat around him. "Talk," Fargo growled and saw Ferris throw a helpless shrug at Myrna.

"I've been stealing from Abelson Shipping for the past ten years," Ferris said with a deep sigh. "In my position I could switch bills, change invoices, pocket the difference. But I needed someone else outside to make it work so I got me a partner, Harry Ross in shipping. We put aside a lot of money over the past ten years."

"And you and your partner decided to take your shares and run," Fargo offered. "But Abelson Shipping found out."

"Not exactly. I decided I'd done all the important work over the years and the money was really mine. I took it from where we'd hidden it and sent it to Snow Bow. Then I quit Abelson's and left."

"With Myrna," Fargo said.

"She was my secretary. She knew everything," Ferris said. "Harry had to find out the money was gone but so was I by then. He couldn't do anything about it. He couldn't go to the sheriff without admitting his own guilt."

"You thought you had everything tied up all neat. Only Harry Ross found out you'd taken the stage for Snow Bow. If he killed just you that might start a lot of questions. But if you were killed in a Crow attack there'd be no questions and he'd have time to track down the money," Fargo said.

"Harry Ross isn't smart enough to plan all that," Ferris said.

"A man gets real smart when he gets real mad," Fargo answered. "It fits." He pushed himself to his feet. "Start walking, the right way this time."

Myrna extended her hand and helped Ferris to his feet. Dripping water with each step, they began to move slowly up the passage and Fargo turned to the others. "In twos, ten yards apart, remember," he said. Charity, holding Mitchell by the hand, started off first, and a few minutes later Marge and Pauline began the climb.

"Lean when it's time to lean," Marge said, pausing before him. "You really meant that, didn't you?"

"I did," Fargo said, his voice hard.

"No matter how rough," she said.

"Rough doesn't count. Truth does," Fargo said and his eyes echoed the hardness in his voice.

Marge went on and Fargo waited to let her and Pauline put on enough distance, then motioned to Holman as he started up the passage. The sun appeared as the gray storm clouds blew away and when Fargo reached the tunnel of rock with Holman the air had already begun to turn warm and the sun baked down. It would take a full day for the mud of the passage to harden back into firm soil, though, he knew. "The ladies can take the sun and dry off at the far end of the tunnel. The men at this end," he said and strode into the sun. He shed his raingear and found himself surprisingly dry underneath, sat down and watched Holman and Ferris take their bags from the stage and pull off their soaked clothes.

Fargo let a little over an hour go by, enough to dry bodies if not clothes and he walked through the tunnel to the other end. "Coming out," he called

125

and saw Charity quickly buttoning a dress as he stepped into the sun. "You can hang wet clothes out on the coach," he said. "We've a few hours of day left. Let's use them." He turned his gaze out across the hills as the women started back into the tunnel. He took in the heavy tree cover but he spotted enough deer trails to follow through the thickest sections. He made a mental note to check out a distant place where the land began to dip downward, turned and strolled back into the tunnel where he'd left the Ovaro. "Want to ride with me awhile, Mitchell?" he asked as he passed the boy and was joined instantly by the small form.

Mitchell sitting in front of him, he led the stage out of the rock tunnel and along the path that grew thick with overhanging hawthorn. "Are we home free, Fargo?" Mitchell asked.

" 'Fraid not. Whoever's chasing us will keep coming. But it'll take them an extra day to find that we took the passage in the storm and every day gets you closer to your grandpa," Fargo said. Mitchell made a happy noise and leaned against him as he sent the Ovaro down a moose trail that proved wide enough for the stage. The trail opened up in a small, grassy knoll bordered by Rocky Mountain maple and wild black cherry on all sides and he halted as dusk swept down. The stage rolled up and he had Marge pull alongside the far edge of the trees. Mitchell swung to the ground with him and Fargo pointed to the wild cherry as the others clambered out of the coach. "Eat plenty of the cherry and save your food. I'll have to shoot us a rabbit soon," he said and saw Delwin Ferris step forward,

Myrna beside him. The man swept everyone with a nervous glance, accusation in his eyes as they passed Fargo and returned to the others.

"I know what you're all thinking," he said. "Fargo's got you convinced they'll kill all of you to get me. But he's wrong. I tell you Harry Ross isn't behind it. He could never dream up anything as clever as that fake Crow attack."

"Delwin's right," Myrna chimed in. "Harry Ross is a stupid plodder." She turned to look at Fargo as the others waited.

"Maybe," he grunted. "And maybe not."

"What are you going to do?" Ferris asked nervously, his eyes searching the big man's impassive countenance. "You can't just toss me out," he blurted.

"Wrong again," Fargo snapped harshly and Ferris swallowed hard.

"Is that what you're going to do?" Myrna asked.

"Didn't say that. I don't know what I'm going to do yet," Fargo answered. "But you'll be the first to know." Myrna turned away, took Ferris by the arm and the man followed with short, shuffling steps. Fargo began to take his bedroll from the Ovaro and Marge came over to him.

"I take it you're satisfied he's the one they're after," she said.

"He fits," Fargo said. "The reasons are all there."

She eyed him impatiently. "You've a way of giving answers that don't really answer," she said.

"You've a way of asking questions that make me wonder," he said.

"Go to hell," she snapped and stalked away. He

uttered a wry sound and started for the trees when he saw the slender form move toward him. Charity's haze-blue eyes were grave, her face set severely.

"Can I talk to you after Mitchell's asleep?" she asked.

"I'll be here," Fargo said.

"Where?"

He gestured into the trees just in front of where the Ovaro was tethered. "Somewhere back there," he said. She nodded, turned and stalked away; he halted at a wild cherry tree, filled his pockets with the fruit and went into the maples. He found a spot where the overhead leaves thinned out and let in the moon, sat down and slowly enjoyed the sweet but slightly puckish fruit. Rum cherries, the old New Englanders called them, because they used the crushed cherries to mellow rum. He pulled off jacket, shirt and gunbelt when he finished, left his trousers on and stretched out as the moon rose high in cream-white fullness.

He heard the sound of brush being pushed aside, footsteps moving through the woods, pausing, starting up again. "Over here," he called and heard the footsteps change direction. Charity came into view, a willowy shape bending under a low branch to halt before him as he rose to his feet. He saw her eyes flick across the smooth, muscled beauty of his torso but her slender face stayed set and the haze-blue eyes held anger. "You wanted to talk to me," he said.

"Yes. I'm really sorry about the bracelet. I was wrong, stupid not to tell you but you don't have to treat me like an outcast because of it," she said, her lips tight. "You haven't said one word to me since it happened. You've not even looked at me."

"Didn't have anything to say," Fargo answered and saw the haze-blue eyes suddenly soften.

"I know why you're here," she said.

"Meaning what?" he frowned.

"Mitchell told me why you agreed to take the stage through," she said.

Fargo made a face. "That was supposed to be between us," he muttered.

"I know but it was right after you saved him. We were talking and he wanted to tell me how really wonderful you were and it just came out," Charity said.

He shrugged. "I figured the kid deserved a break," he said.

"I said you were made of contradictions. I was more right than I imagined. The way you made Ferris talk was brutal and ruthless yet you're risking your neck to see a little boy reaches his grandfather," Charity said.

"You saying you can accept a saint and a sinner all in one package?" Fargo grinned.

"I guess so," she answered. "I know you said that'd mean I'd have to take another look at myself."

"Have you?" he questioned.

"Maybe," Charity murmured.

He reached an arm out, curled a hand behind her neck and felt the smoothness of her skin under the dark blond hair. He drew her to him, slowly, gently. "How much of a look?" he asked and her haze-blue eyes were suddenly smoky.

"I don't know," Charity breathed and he felt her

129

stiffen. He bent down, pressed his lips to hers. She held back, unmoving, until suddenly he felt softness come to her lips and she returned the kiss, lingered and he pressed his mouth harder. "Oh," she breathed as he pressed her lips open and she felt his tongue slide forward, touch her lips, move tantalizingly. "Oh," she breathed again and her hands pressed into the bare skin of his chest. "I don't know," she murmured. "I don't know." But he felt her hands move along his skin, press, feel, rub and he pulled at the top of her dress and the buttons came open with a rush.

He touched very smooth skin, curled his fingers down around the cup of one modest breast and let his thumb touch the tiny nipple. "Oh, oh, no . . . no, oh, I don't know," Charity gasped but she didn't draw away and her hands dug into his chest. He pulled at the buttons again and the dress fell open and slid down to the ground. He pushed down underclothes, swung her up in his arms and put her on the bedroll as she clung to him. "Wait, oh, wait," Charity pleaded and he moved back, his hands on her shoulders as the haze-blue eyes stared up at him.

"Whatever you say, honey," he murmured softly and let himself take in the beauty of her—slender, willowy body, small waist and the modest breasts beautifully curved with tiny pink nipples on tiny pink areolas. A flat abdomen went into a slightly curved belly, flat hips and a small, pristine triangle of tiny black tendrils. Nice legs that just avoided being thin were held tightly together as she buried her face into his chest to avoid his eyes that took in her loveliness. He let his hand run down her back and she gave a soft cry that grew sharp as he bent down, brought her head up and pressed his mouth over hers. He pulled on her lips, pressed her mouth open, explored, and she responded with a movement of suddenness, then drew back with equal suddenness to stare up at him.

"I don't know," she murmured, her lips parted and the haze-blue eyes darkened. He let one hand cup her left breast, gently rubbed his thumb across the tiny nipple, rubbed it again and Charity's back arched under his other hand. "Oh, my God, oh, oh my," she breathed and he bent down, closed his lips gently around the soft-firm breast, caressing the nipple with his tongue. "Oooooh, oh, oooooh," Charity breathed. "No, no," she gasped out as her hands came up to clasp the back of his neck and press him into her. He sucked, caressed, felt the pink tip grow under his lips, become firm, a surrogate invitation to his own burgeoning, pulsating growth. He slipped his Levi's off as he kept gently sucking on her breast and she gave out short half-cries of protest and pleasure mixed together.

He pressed her down, brought his body against her and felt the hot, throbbing maleness that was his push into her belly. "Ah, ah . . . aaaaah, no, no, oh, God," Charity cried out and her head rolled from side to side as he lay atop her. He let flesh seduce flesh, warmth penetrate warmth, and he slowly put his hand down over the hardly raised pubic mound and she cried out again. He reached lower, probed, dipped into the dark places and felt the moistness of her thighs. He rested, gently pushed again and the long legs parted, came together over his hand, quivered, then parted again. He touched, gently, and felt the quiver course through her. He waited, let her gather desire, touched the soft, lusciously smooth lips, parted the warm and wanting flesh and heard Charity's scream, a cry of wanting that refused the protest of words. He stroked, caressed, touched, and Charity's legs flew open and her back arched as she screamed. He shifted, brought his own warm, eager, throbbing instrument to rest at the very tip of her moist portal.

"Oh, God, iiiiiieeee." Charity cried out, arched up and sank her heels onto the bedroll and drove forward. He felt the tight warmth of her seize him, expand, give way and he heard her cry of pain and pleasure again. He slid forward and she clasped her legs around him, lifted her slender body to cling to him with arms and legs as he filled her completely, pressed against the very end of the warm, wet, pulsating sleeve. "Oh, oh, oh, oh," she gasped out in tiny breaths as he moved inside her, pushed back and forth and felt the pleasure of her as she stayed tight around him, the frictionless friction of ecstasy encompassing him.

Charity was making tiny sighing sounds against his shoulder as she sank down onto the bedroll with him, her back arching, falling, arching again. Now her legs moved up and down his own as she rubbed every part of herself against him in rhythm with his slow thrustings.

"Oh, oh, oh, my God," Charity cried out suddenly and again her head rolled from side to side. He felt her hands suddenly pushing hard against his chest as though trying to get away while her legs clamped around his waist. "No, no, no ... aaaaiiiii, oh, my God," she screamed and he felt her quivering explosion engulf him and he let himself come with her and her scream curled high into the trees. When her cry quivered into silence she stayed against him, holding him tight. Finally, with a quick, gasped breath, she let go and fell back, her arms falling outward as if in defeat.

Fargo settled beside her, leaned over and gently kissed each beautifully shaped, modest breast. Her hand curled around his neck, drawing him to her. "I wondered," she murmured. "Ever since you saved Mitchell. Maybe before."

"Wondered what?"

"How much sinner there was in me," she said.

"Enough," Fargo laughed. "But then I see this as more saintly than sinful."

Her smile held an edge of uncertainty and she pushed herself up on her elbows. "This could be habit-forming, whichever it is," she said.

"Could be," he agreed.

"I have to get back. I don't want Mitchell waking up with questions," Charity said and started to wriggle into her clothes. When she finished, she paused, her haze-blue eyes grave. "There's one thing more," she said. "Seeing as how it's truth time, inner and outer. I didn't tell you the whole truth about getting Mitchell to his grandfather by the fifteenth. I was promised fifty dollars for every day I got him there before the fifteenth."

Fargo turned the admission in his mind. "I'm glad you told me." He smiled. "But it doesn't exactly put you in a class with Ferris."

"Good," Charity murmured as she leaned against him. "I'm glad I came to talk to you."

"You can come for this kind of talk anytime," Fargo said. She pushed away, frowned up at him.

"What about Marge O'Day?" she questioned.

His smile was laced with ruefulness. "Marge isn't happy with me. I'm thinking she's holding something back, too," he said. "I'd guess a lot more than you."

Charity brushed his cheek with her lips as she turned and hurried away and he waited till he could no longer hear her in the brush before he lay down, stretched out and his lips turned tight. Charity had been an unexpected and welcome moment but her question about Marge had brought reality back. He had to decide what to do about Ferris and he'd have another day to do it at best. The man's admission made him the target, despite his denials. It all fit, Fargo grunted as he closed his eyes and drew sleep around him. Almost all of it.

6

Fargo held the Ovaro atop the high ledge as he peered back across the thick, lush terrain. Below, the coach moved through a trail he'd found after the deer and moose trails wore away. He'd kept a hard pace through the day and by tomorrow afternoon they'd reach the place where the mountains began to dip downward in a long green slope. But his jaw set tight as he peered into the distance and saw the tree branches move in an almost straight line.

"Damn," he muttered. They were close, too close. They'd done hard riding to catch up this soon. But the night was only another hour away. They'd make camp and come charging before the morning was old. He wheeled the pinto around and sent the horse down a steep slope that brought him to the trail below as the stage rolled up. He motioned to a wide space between two white birch and dismounted as Marge drove the stage into the spot. Earlier in the day he'd shot two big blacktailed jackrabbits and given them to Pauline when she told him she'd skinned more rabbits than he'd ever seen. Now he saw Pauline swing from the coach, the skinned rabbits in hand.

"Ready for roasting," she announced proudly. He had Mitchell gather firewood while he fashioned a crude spit from a length of birch and set the rabbits to cook. He saw fear and worry in the quick glances Delwin Ferris threw at him but he sat back and said nothing until the rabbits were roasted and eaten hungrily and the fire began to burn out.

"We're going to do some fighting come morning," he said.

"With what? You've got the only guns," Holman said.

"I'm going to get us some guns right now and I'll tell you how you're going to use them in the morning," Fargo said.

"Am I included?" Ferris asked.

"For now," Fargo said.

"Does that mean you don't think they're really after him?" Holman questioned.

"No, it means I need him to fire a gun. I don't think they'll just kill him and leave the rest of us," Fargo snapped. "Now get yourselves some sleep. I'll be back but you won't know it."

He rose and Charity came to him. "Be careful," she murmured. "Without you there's no chance of making it."

"Things haven't changed there," he grunted.

"Some things have. They only need you. I want you." She smiled slyly.

He brushed his hand lightly over one breast as he turned away and swung onto the Ovaro. "See you

136

come morning," he said and sent the horse southward through the forests. He paused frequently to draw the night wind into his nostrils and, finally smelling the scent of campfire, turned the horse to follow his nose. The odor of the fire grew stronger quickly and he slowed when he saw the soft glow of embers still burning, went on another fifty yards and slid to the ground. He moved quickly on foot, steps light and catlike, and approached the edge of the camp in minutes. The sleeping forms lay scattered around the fire. They'd posted no sentries, confident they needed none. Exactly as he had expected, he smiled to himself and began to edge around the campsite to where the horses were tethered. He counted the sleeping figures as he moved and totaled sixteen forms. The horses moved, whinnied as he reached them, instantly aware of a stranger. He froze, his eyes on the figures on the ground. But no one woke and he placed a hand soothingly on the rump of the nearest horse until the animal quieted.

The rifle case hung from the rear of the saddle and he quietly slid the rifle out, saw it was a .44 Henry and tucked it under his arm. He stepped to the next horse and slid the gun from the rifle case and went on to the next until he had all he could carry without fear of dropping one. With three under each arm he moved from the horses and lay the rifles down on the grass, turned and went back to the rest of the horses. Working with stealth, he pulled each rifle from its case, removed over half the shells and returned the gun. When he finished, his pockets heavy with ammunition, he picked up the six rifles on the grass and silently made his way back to the Ovaro.

It was unlikely they'd check their rifles in the morning but anyone who did would see the shells he'd left in each gun and be satisfied. They'd all find the unhappy surprise waiting for them when they started shooting. Fargo rode unhurriedly back to the stage, tethered the Ovaro and put his back against a birch and slept at once. When the new day came on streaks of yellow and pink, he woke, washed and waited for the others to emerge. He had the rifles standing against a tree when they gathered around and he handed one to each person except Mitchell, giving each an extra handful of shells. "I never fired a rifle before," Charity said.

"You point it at somebody and pull the trigger," Fargo said. "I don't expect you to be sharpshooters. The important thing is to shoot, as fast and as straight as you can."

"I'll get at least one, I promise you," Pauline said and he believed her.

"You'll be inside the coach," he told her. "You too, Myrna. You'll sit on the driver's seat beside Marge, Ferris," he added and saw the surprise come into the man's face.

"So they'll see me?" He frowned.

"You get the cigar," Fargo said.

"That's making me a target," Ferris protested.

"You are a target. We all are. Be glad you're getting a chance to fight back," Fargo said coldly. "Now get your lying ass up on that seat." He surveyed the others as Ferris climbed onto the stage, Marge watching him with her eyes narrowed. "You'll hear them come charging up from behind. The minute you do you rein up, jump down and fire from beneath the stage," he said to Marge and took Ferris in with his glance. "Until then you walk the horses real slow. The rest of us will be in the trees on both sides of you." He turned to Holman and Charity. "You two in the trees on that side," he ordered. "Mitchell will stay with me on this side. We'll walk a dozen yards behind in the trees. That way they'll be between us as they charge up to the stage. You start shooting the minute I do. Everything clear?"

The others nodded, none happily, and Fargo pointed to the thick trees across the trail; Charity started toward them with Holman behind her. "Roll," Fargo said and Marge pulled the coach from between the birches and onto the trail. She walked the team slowly, he saw. One hand on Mitchell's shoulder, he moved into the dense trees and began to follow, staying a good dozen yards back. "We'll have a surprise for them," Mitchell said eagerly.

"More than one. Their rifles are more than half empty," Fargo said and Mitchell chortled in glee. Fargo glanced back at the Ovaro as the horse followed through the trees and was satisfied the foliage was thick enough to hide him from sight. He guessed they had walked perhaps an hour when he felt the tremor in the ground, first, then picked up the sound of galloping hoofs. It'd be another minute before Marge picked up the sound, he was certain, and he motioned to Mitchell as he halted and the boy dropped to one knee. The sound of hoofbeats was suddenly loud and Fargo saw Marge glance back, her eyes wide, as she yanked the team to a halt.

The riders came into sight, charging hard at the stage, rifles out and ready. Fargo shot a glance at Marge and Ferris and saw Marge already halfway down from the driver's seat. Ferris, his rifle held awkwardly under his arm, had trouble clambering from the stage. Fargo brought the big Sharps up as he saw the first two attackers start to raise their rifles. He fired, two shots in rapid succession, and the two men toppled almost as one, both falling headfirst from their mounts. The rifle fire erupted from the trees at the other side and he glimpsed Pauline firing from the window of the coach. He got off a shot at another attacker who tried to squeeze past the stage and the man screamed in pain as he fell from his horse.

The attackers had fired off their first two rounds as they reined up in confusion. Fargo saw another go down as he slammed a bullet into a man on a short-legged mare and the figure almost somersaulted out of the saddle as his chest sprayed red. "God-damn," he heard one of the men shout as he found his rifle clicking empty. "Shit," another swore as his gun failed to fire. Fargo got off two more shots and heard Pauline firing furiously. Two more figures fell as the others wheeled in a moment of confusion and then began to race away. Fargo lowered the big Sharps and heard Holman and Charity firing wildly at the fleeing horsemen. He rose to his feet, looked down at Mitchell who got up with his eyes wide.

"One more for our side," he said and Mitchell's

face broke into a gleeful smile. Fargo kept the rest of his thoughts to himself but he knew they'd been lucky once again and that luck had a way of running out.

He pushed out of the trees onto the trail and watched Charity emerge from the other side, Holman close behind her and he saw her eyes go to Mitchell at once as she breathed a sigh of relief.

"They just broke off and hightailed it," Pauline said from the stage.

"They found themselves bushwhacked and their rifles empty. I'd run, too," Fargo said and Pauline smiled appreciatively as she nodded. Fargo scanned the still forms scattered along the trail. "They won't be telling us anything," he muttered. "Let's roll." He climbed onto the pinto and saw Ferris pulling himself onto the stage, perspiring profusely as Myrna helped him up.

"You think they'll come after us again?" Holman asked.

"I'd say so. They're hired guns and they've got enough men left for another try," Fargo said.

"Goddamn you, Ferris, this is all your fault," Holman snapped as he climbed into the stage. "You've no right being here with us."

"I'm here and you keep your mouth shut," Ferris shouted defensively.

"Save your breath, both of you," Fargo called out. "Roll that stage." Marge snapped the reins and the team pulled forward as he sent the Ovaro past the coach and down the trail. The trees grew in to leave little room but the coach managed to scrape through and he rode ahead, explored, found a very shallow but wide stream that coursed downhill and had the stage roll on in the stream. It served as a watery trail and let the horses cool their feet until it came to an abrupt end in a small pool that formed at the base of a rock formation. He dismounted and called a rest as he scanned the area. The rocks and the pool formed a strange little oasis of granite in the midst of the lush, green hills and he took his canteen and slid down against one of the flat-sided stones.

He watched Charity stroll over to him and lower herself to the ground beside him with a speculative gaze. "Something's bothering you," she commented and he smiled.

"You guessing or saying?" he asked.

"Saying. It's in your eyes," Charity said. "Restless, troubled."

He cocked his head at her and his smile stayed. "Maybe," he allowed. She waited and his gaze swept the others as they rested, sipped water from the pool, wiped perspiration from their faces. "I figured those sidewinders would be out to get all of us but they had to see Ferris. Somebody should've made a special effort to get him but nobody did. There's something more that keeps digging at me. Zeb Jonah said the man pulling the strings was called Tex. Ferris's partner was Harry Ross."

"What are you saying?" Charity asked.

"There's maybe more than one rotten apple in the barrel," Fargo murmured. "I'm going to find out right now." Charity frowned and Fargo nodded to the rock just above where Cyrus Holman sat on the ground and mopped his face with a kerchief.

142

She let out a tiny gasp as she saw the diamondback curled at the edge of the rock.

"You wouldn't," she whispered.

"Watch," he growled as he rose, picked up a piece of branch on the ground and casually climbed higher on the rocks. He paused as Myrna looked at him, bent down and seemed to examine a growth of orange star lichen on the rocks. When she looked away he edged sideways, closer to the rattler. He stayed a foot above where the snake lay coiled but as he neared it he saw the rattler's head lift as it sensed danger. He glanced down at the others again. They were all occupied except for Charity, whose eyes were riveted on him. He took a firmer grasp on the end of the branch, edged a few inches closer to the snake, gauged the short distance again and snapped the branch out in a lightning-quick motion. He flipped the big diamondback into the air and over the edge, yanking the Colt from its holster while the snake was still falling.

The rattler landed exactly where he expected it to land, right in front of Holman, curled into its striking position instantly, rattling furiously. Fargo saw Holman's face drain of color as he stared at the big snake at his feet. "Don't move," Fargo called. "I've got a bead on him."

"Shoot, for Christ's sake, shoot," Holman rasped. The rattler flicked its tongue out, rattled more furiously as its glass-bead eyes stared at the figure in front of it. "Shoot," Holman breathed in a hoarse whisper.

"A man faces death it makes him remember things," Fargo said.

"Shoot." Holman gagged and his face was suddenly wet with perspiration.

"What's the real reason you're on this stage, Holman?" Fargo said as he kept the rattler in his sights.

"You crazy?" Holman breathed. "Shoot. God, shoot."

"I could miss. I can't concentrate when I think I've been lied to," Fargo said and saw the diamondback coil itself a fraction tighter. He knew what that meant. The snake was getting ready to strike.

"All right, Jesus, all right," Holman gasped out. "Shoot, for God's sake."

Fargo saw the snake's head move almost imperceptibly and he knew the moment had come. He pulled the trigger back as the rattler struck and saw the shot slam into the snake's head with an explosion of blood, skin and bones. The body of the big diamondback lashed and twitched on the ground, a headless reflex, and then lay still. Fargo saw Holman topple onto his side, his breath coming in long gasps. Casually, the big man dropped down from the rock and reached down, pulled Holman to a sitting position and propped him against the rock. Holman stared up at him, his face dripping with perspiration, a mixture of awe and disbelief in his eyes. He licked his sand-dry lips as he brought words up from deep inside him.

"Sam Waterton," Holman said. "I sold him a load of bad medicine that wiped out his whole herd, put him out of business. Same thing happened with two other cattlemen, and I decided to run for it. They swore to kill me, swore it in front of a saloon full of people. I figured they'd realize they were as good as convicted if they killed me."

"Not if you were killed as part of a Crow attack or in a dry-gulching that killed everybody else," Fargo said. Holman stared at him and finally looked away. "You fit, Holman, every bit as well as Ferris does, maybe better," Fargo said.

"You've your damn nerve yelling at me, Holman," Ferris cut in.

"You both lied," Fargo barked and strode away, paused, turned back to Holman. "Those three cattlemen, any of them named Tex?" he asked.

Holman shrugged helplessly. "I don't know. Maybe as a nickname. I don't know," he said. Fargo nodded and accepted the answer. Holman had always been a hollow man and now he was drained, beyond lying anymore. "Let's roll. We've daylight left," Fargo said and watched Marge climb onto the driver's seat, her face pulled tight, her lips a thin, almost bloodless line. Fargo took the Ovaro on ahead of the coach, pushing through a trail that grew thick with vines and he slowed and watched the stage pull its way through the clutching growths. He rode on and found a steep passage wide enough for the stage as it led downward. He halted as the coach came along and swung from the Ovaro to the driver's seat beside Pauline. Marge glanced at him with surprise. "You can hold the team back if I can keep the handbrake on real tight," he said.

"I'll take the reins for the second brace," Pauline said and Fargo agreed with a nod. He closed his hand around the handbrake and pulled back as Marge sent the team down the steep passage. Instantly, he felt the tremendous pull on arm and shoulder muscles, then on the tendons in his hand, as the brake ground against the wheels of the coach. He smelled the acrid odor of wood burning under the tremendous friction and it seemed that his shoulder muscles were about to burst, but he held the brake against the wheels until they reached the bottom of the passage.

"Whoa," Marge called as she yanked the reins back and Pauline did the same. The coach rolled to a halt and Fargo grimaced in pain as he forced his hand open, each finger curled in stiffness. He let his arm hang down until the blood circulated freely again and strained and cramped muscles returned to normal.

Dust had begun to filter down and he motioned to a glen of alders a half-dozen yards on. Marge pulled the stage into the glen and Fargo followed, examined the shoe of the handbrake and saw the charred and shredded wood, only enough left for ordinary use. He was still examining the brake when Marge came up to him and her eyes gazed out across the land as she spoke to him.

"How much longer to Snow Bow?" she asked.

"Without trouble, maybe two, three days," Fargo said. He pointed to where the land dipped down in the distance and the purple settled over the terrain. "That way, due north," he said and she nodded.

"Maybe there won't be any more trouble," she said.

"Don't bet on it," Fargo grunted and she turned away and took a strip of beef jerky from her traveling bag. Night settled in fast and Charity came to him as the moon began to lift its way high into the blue-velvet sky.

"Where will I find you tonight?" she murmured.

"Noplace," he said and drew a glance of surprise. "Nothing personal," he said.

"You expect trouble tonight?" she persisted.

"Maybe," he allowed and Charity knew she'd not pull anything more from him. She brushed his cheek with her lips and moved away, letting her body sway with willowy grace. He smiled after her. He took the Ovaro and went into the trees as the pale light filtered down. He gazed back through the forest, drew a mental line north from the camp and moved on again until he finally halted in a dark, dense cluster of maple. He sat down, settled back against a tree trunk and let his eyes close. The night sounds were magnified instantly without the distraction of seeing, and he rested and let the minute roll past.

He waited, silently, patiently but he finally began to think that he had perhaps guessed wrong. He contemplated opening his eyes when suddenly the soft night sounds were interrupted by the sound of a horse moving almost at a gallop.

He rose to his feet at once, stayed in the dense, dark thicket, and the figure came into view, a dozen yards to the right, riding hard through the trees. The moonlight caught the tinted blond hair and outlined the large breasts as she raced past the thicket of maples and he let her go on before pulling himself into the saddle. She'd unhitched one of the team horses, taken the rifle and her bag and walked the horse until she was far enough from the campsite to ride and now she raced through the night. Fargo sent the pinto after her, saw her swerve through trees, riding almost out of control and much too fast for the darkness and for terrain she didn't know.

He hung back, waited for her to slow but she kept the horse thundering through low brush, narrowly missing trees. Fargo's eyes peered beyond the racing horse, and the moonlight touched the tops of trees that suddenly dropped to the left. He laid a hand on the Ovaro's neck and the horse took on more speed at once. Marge had disappeared from sight for a moment but Fargo's gaze went to the trees ahead and saw they dropped off more sharply than they'd appeared to from a distance. He'd gone another dozen yards when he heard the sharp cry and the sound of a horse stumbling, falling, landing heavily in brush and low ground cover. He slowed the pinto and moved carefully forward and saw where the land began to drop off sharply, the trees following the terrain.

In racing headlong through the night, Marge had completely missed seeing the land change, the sharp drop appear, until it was too late. Fargo reined up and peered down and saw the horse get to its feet, snort and shake itself. Marge lay on the ground on her back and he watched as she slowly raised her head, pushed up on her elbows. "Goddamn," he heard her curse and knew she was more bruised and shaken than hurt. Slowly, he eased the pinto down the sharp drop, let the horse take the incline sideways and saw Marge look up as she used a low branch to pull herself to her feet. He halted in front of her, saw the bruise on her cheek, a small cut on her forehead and the tinted blond hair hanging in disarray with leaves clinging to it.

He dismounted and went to the horse, ran his hands over each leg, checked fetlocks and pasterns, knees and brisket. "What about me?" Marge bit out.

"This horse has to pull a stage. You don't," Fargo said and straightened up. "He's all right. I'll take him back."

"Take him back?" Marge frowned.

Fargo turned, let his eyes bore ice into her. "You were so damned anxious to run. You can keep on running, on foot, now," he said.

"I ran because I know you've been wondering about me. I didn't want to be next," she said.

"You ran because you didn't want to tell me the truth. You lied just like the others lied," Fargo said coldly. "Now you've got a choice. You can start talking or start walking."

Her eyes searched his face and he knew she'd see only the unyielding harshness of his words. Her large breasts rose high as she drew in a deep breath and let it out in a long sigh of defeat. "The owner of the last place I worked was in love with me. He promised me everything I wanted only he was a madman, a crazy, wild, insanely jealous madman. He shot two men because he didn't like the way they looked at me," Marge said. "When I said I wanted to leave he threatened to kill me and he wouldn't give me any of the back pay I'd let accumulate. He thought that'd keep me there with him."

"Seems he was wrong," Fargo commented.

"That's right. I cleaned out his safe, everything coming to me and a lot more," Marge said. "I heard he went absolutely crazy. I hid out and then took the stage for Snow Bow. It seemed plenty far enough away from him."

Fargo's eyes were narrowed in thought as she finished. "It fits, as well as any of the others," he said. "A jilted lover, crazed with jealousy but smart enough to know he'd be the number-one suspect if only you were killed."

Marge shrugged and looked pained. "He's insane enough and smart enough to cook up anything," she said.

Fargo's eyes were harsh as he peered at her. "You knew it all along and you kept your mouth shut. You lied just like Ferris and Holman. You're no better than they are," he said, spun on his heel and swung onto the Ovaro. He took the team horse in tow and began to make his way along the bottom of the slope as Marge followed with the rifle and her bag. He heard her stumble, fall and struggle up as he kept moving on. He didn't look back and found where the sharp drop tapered off and started up to the higher ground.

Marge had fallen far behind but he could still hear her stumbling through the brush. He paused when he reached the top and let her catch up enough to glimpse him through the trees as he rode on. He reached the campsite, had the horse hitched back in the shafts when she trudged up and glared at him. "Bastard. You could've let me ride," she hissed.

"You could've told me the truth from the start,"

Fargo snapped and brushed past her. He went into the trees just past the glen, pulled off clothes and let sleep come to wash away the sour taste in his mouth. It was still there, though, he found when morning came and he waited until the others were dressed and ready to move before he halted in front of them.

"Heard you at the horses last night," Holman said. "Something wrong?"

"Marge, here, decided to cut out on her own. She changed her mind, though," Fargo said and drew a glower from the wide face. "You and Ferris have company, Holman. It seems Marge could be why somebody wants us all wiped out," Fargo went on and saw Ferris and Holman stare at Marge with instant frowns. "This is no stage to Snow Bow. It's a stagecoach to hell because of one of you," Fargo said. "I'm thinking of going on with Charity, Pauline and Mitchell and leaving the rest of you here."

"You can't do that," Ferris said. "Only one of us is guilty."

"Wrong," Fargo barked. "Only one of you is responsible but you're all guilty. Each of you knew what you running from and you lied by keeping quiet about it. The only reason I don't leave you is because I want to find out which of you I'm going to turn in when this is over. Now let's roll." He turned away, pulled himself onto the Ovaro, took a moment to wave at Mitchell and rode on through the trees. He found little places for the stage to thread its way through the woods and by afternoon they'd reached the place where the land dipped downward and became a long, green slope of mostly thick mountain bromegrass. They'd gone halfway down the long slope when he halted to rest the horses at a small stream that cut diagonally across the ground.

Charity came alongside him as he refilled his canteen. "We still being followed?" she asked. "I've noticed you keep checking behind us."

"I'd bet on it. But they're being more careful. I haven't been able to spot them," he said.

Her hand touched his arm, a soft pressure. "Are you going to be busy again tonight?" she asked.

"Tell you later," he said and drew a half-pout from her as she returned to the stage. Fargo took to the saddle again and his eyes swept the top of the slope. There was not much place to stay in cover on the slope and he saw no signs of horsemen following. They could halt at the edge of the slope and hang back and watch, he realized, and he muttered oaths under his breath as he rode on.

The day was drawing to an end when they reached the bottom of the long slope and the land leveled off with stands of alder and mountain ash almost alternating. There was still an hour of daylight left when he halted the stage alongside a nest of mountain ash.

He turned away at once and rode back along the line of trees that bordered the edge of the long slope. They could have watched from the very top and taken a long, circling path around the edge of the slope. But they'd have lost hours and that didn't set right. Even so, they hadn't broken off the chase, not after all the planning and determined pursuit they'd put into it. That was even less likely. Fargo finally turned back and felt a gnawing uneasiness inside himself. Dark had settled in when he reached the stage and the little group was just finishing their meal. "This is the last of the food we've brought," Myrna said to him. "Perhaps you could bring down another jackrabbit tomorrow."

"We'll likely make Snow Bow in another two days," Fargo said. "A little fasting is good for the soul."

"You are a bastard," Marge snapped. "You're penalizing all of us because you don't know who's guilty."

"Maybe I'll find you some fruit along the way," Fargo said as he sat down at the side of a tall ash and saw Charity appear and slide down beside him.

"She's half-right," Charity said. "You are being a bit harsh."

"I've enough jerky in my saddlebag for you, Mitchell and Pauline," he said.

"I should've known," Charity said. "And I'm still waiting for an answer to what I asked you by the stream."

He paused as the uneasiness pulled at him. He was being foolish, he told himself. They wouldn't try a night attack. They were no trackers or trappers skilled in the ways of silence and stealth. They were a pack of hired killers and they knew their limitations. They knew they could never sneak up silently through the brush. They'd strike by day, in the ways that were best for them, he told himself. He looked down at Charity and felt the warm waiting of her, haze-blue eyes filled with promise. "Back there through those two trees," he said and she hurried silently away with a tiny smile edging her lips.

He took his bedroll down and went into the forest, found a spot beside a pair of saplings and took off his gunbelt and shirt. He stretched out and muttered a curse at the uneasiness that refused to go away. He lay still and waited and the damn uneasiness only persisted. It nagged, irritated, a tiny voice whispering that something was wrong, something his logic had missed. Dammit, what was keeping her, he swore silently. A pair of warm and willing legs would be more than normally welcome tonight, he muttered and sat up as he saw Charity's figure appear through the trees. "Sorry I took so long," she said as she came down beside him, pressed her mouth to his, her lips soft, wet, sweet.

"Mitchell have trouble getting to sleep?" Fargo asked and lay back.

"No, not Mitchell, the others were restless. I managed to sneak around the back of the stage and tiptoe my way," Charity said. "The advantages of being alone and light-footed." She flicked open buttons, wriggled out of the top of the dress and the curved, white breasts turned to him, the tiny, pink tips pointing firmly upward. He stared at the lovely sight as Charity's words hammered in his head. *The advantages of being alone and light-footed.*

"That's it, dammit," he hissed as he bounced up and strapped on his gunbelt with one swift motion. "Get dressed. You're going back," he said as Charity stared at him.

"What is it?" She frowned.

"Change in plans, *their* plans," Fargo muttered.

"Just get your ass back to the stage fast." He yanked her to her feet and her breasts bounced enticingly before she pulled the dress closed.

"I don't understand," she said.

"I'll explain tomorrow," he said. "Now move." She flung a look of dismay at him as she went off through the trees and he waited a moment, gathered his bedroll under one arm and slowly followed. He gave her time to reach the campsite and crawl back to the stage where Mitchell slept. He moved closer and halted inside the trees and flattened himself on his stomach beside a thick ash, the Colt in his hand. Holman lay on the ground near the front wheels of the coach, Pauline in her blanket at the rear left wheel. Marge lay hard asleep halfway under the body of the coach, the others inside. Fargo lay still and cursed at himself. He'd almost made a fatal mistake. They'd decided to try a single assassin this time. That's why he'd picked up no sign that they were following. They'd failed with each attack. Whoever pulled the strings decided it was time to try something else. No more tries at hiding murder with massacre. No more masquerades. Time was running out and success was more important than disguise.

He curled his hand around the butt of the Colt, relaxed his fingers and swept the sleeping figures with a slow glance, brought his eyes to the trees beyond. There was no need to strain to see. The killer would have to come into the open. Besides, he'd hear him, first, Fargo was certain and he put his head down on the ground, closed his eyes and let his wild-creature hearing turn the night sounds into pictures. Deer in the distance to the right, the soft swooshing swoop of bats, the humming of insects, the zigzag rush of air that was the nighthawk's flight, the staccato click of beetles, everything in its place, everything with its own signature of sound.

As the night wore on nothing came to inject itself into the night sounds and only the soft wind moved the leaves of tree and bush. Maybe he'd jumped to conclusions, he found himself wondering as the moon began to curve down at the far end of the sky. He'd let logic sway him first, then instinct, and he always placed more faith in instinct. Logic and reason were building blocks. They often seemed right when they weren't and you only found out when the house collapsed. Instinct was pure, direct and, if you didn't let logic get in its way, it was damn near always right. He shut off thoughts and concentrated on the night sounds again.

Perhaps another hour had passed, the moon almost out of sight near the horizon line, when he heard the faint sound of careful footsteps. He lifted his head, snapped his eyes open. The wind had carried the sound from the trees across from him and he waited, his finger curling around the trigger of the Colt. The figure appeared, moving slowly into the open ground in a half-crouch. The man stepped carefully toward the stage and the last of the moon caught the dull glint of the gun in his right hand.

Fargo watched, his lips drawn tight, and let the figure move closer to the stage. The man would give him the answers he wanted when he singled out his target. It'd be a matter of split seconds after that, Fargo realized. When the man found his target he'd shoot and run. He'd have to shoot first, Fargo knew, seize that fleeting instant between the time the killer saw his target and pressed the trigger. He could call out, he knew, but that would only explode in an exchange of gunfire and he'd learn nothing. He drew his lips back. He'd play it to the finish and hope he could seize that single, fleeting instant.

The figure stepped to the edge of the stage and Fargo saw him pause, glance down at Pauline and move on. He slowed as he came to Marge, the gun poised in his hand, ready to fire, and Fargo felt his finger close on the trigger of the big Colt. The man peered hard when suddenly the silence exploded, Mitchell's voice from inside the stage. "Somebody's outside," the boy called and Fargo saw the man whirl, raise the gun to fire. Fargo pressed the trigger and the Colt blasted through the night and the man spun, gagged, clutched at his shoulder. Fargo sprang from the trees, the Colt aimed and ready to fire again.

"Drop the gun," he shouted as the figure, on one knee, held one hand to his shoulder. He saw the man raise his arm, aim his six-gun directly at him. Fargo fired again, two shots this time and the man jerked violently on one knee and, still twitching, fell backward with his legs twisted beneath him. The others had snapped awake, pushed themselves to their feet, and Fargo holstered the Colt as he reached the stage. The man wouldn't be getting up.

The answers he could have given would stay with him forever.

He saw Mitchell, Charity beside him, peer out of the stage. "I woke up. I don't know why, and I saw a man standing there," Mitchell said.

"You did real well, Mitchell," Fargo said as the others stared at the slain intruder.

"You were waiting. You expected this," Marge breathed.

"I got a sudden hunch," Fargo said and saw Charity's little smile. "You can go back to sleep," he said as he began to drag the figure across the ground and into the trees beyond. He searched the man's clothing and found nothing, as he expected would be the case. Hired killers seldom carried anything to mark them. He walked back to the stage, settled down against a tree and slept the few hours left of the night.

When the sun woke him he rose and scanned Ferris and Holman, watched Marge unfold herself from under the coach and Myrna step from the open door. He swore silently and realized he felt cheated. He'd come within a fraction of a second of knowing the answer he wanted and fate had exploded it in his face. He turned his gaze to the long slope behind them and nothing moved. "Let's roll," he said and climbed onto the pinto. He motioned to Mitchell and the boy ran to him, pulling himself into the saddle happily. "If we're lucky, you might get to see your grandpa before the day's out." Fargo said.

"You've got to meet him, Fargo," Mitchell said.

"We'll see," Fargo allowed and sent the Ovaro

down a gentle pass that was soft with forest star moss. The land softened as they moved down from the high hills and trails opened up that let him set a fast pace on mostly downhill terrain. They had crested the last of the middle hills by noon and he found a thick stand of wild pears which were hungrily devoured. He'd watched the land behind throughout the morning and he was finally convinced there'd be no more attacks. No more riders dogged their trail, no horsemen filed silently through the hills. Missoula Snow Bow lay just beyond the line of foothills in front of them, and he swore under his breath. They'd be there before the day ended.

"You're all lucky," he said as they prepared to move on. "It looks as though you're going to make it in one piece."

"That bothers you, doesn't it, Fargo?" Holman said, a sneer in his voice.

"I guess so," Fargo admitted. "I hate to see swindlers, cheats, crooks and liars get off scot-free."

"You're just pissed off because you'll never know which of us almost got everybody else killed," Marge said. "It doesn't matter now. It never did."

"It matters. Truth always matters," he answered and heard the tiredness in his voice. His answer had been more for Mitchell than himself and he sent the pinto on down a wide trail that cut directly through the foothills. He called a halt once more in mid-afternoon with only another hour's ride out of the low hills. Charity came to rest beside him and he saw the haze-blue eyes studying him.

"I'll have time once I turn Mitchell over to his grandfather," she said.

"I'll keep that in mind," he said. "What happens when you reach Snow Bow?"

"There's an inn. I wrote ahead for reservations. I expect somebody will come for us after we get there," she said. "The others are all going to check in there first. I heard them talking about it." She paused and allowed a tiny smile to reach out to him. "I reserved a separate room for Mitchell," she said.

"I'll keep that in mind, too," Fargo said. "Let's move. The sooner we get to town the better." She nodded smugly and hurried to the coach and Fargo sent the pinto on ahead once more, scanned the surrounding land out of habit. But nothing moved and when he reached the bottom of the foothills he glimpsed the buildings in the distance. He waited till the stage caught up to him, waved it on and rode across flat ground toward the town. The buildings took shape as he neared, became warehouses and shed, frame houses and brick structures. Snow Bow had a proper bank, he noted as he rode past it down Main Street, a half-dozen buildings away from the Snow Bow Saloon. He spotted a two-story, white frame building with a board and lodging sign outside and he halted and swung to the ground. The stage drew curious stares as it rolled along the street to a halt, he noted. Snow Bow was a town of Owensboro mountain wagons, of California rack bed rigs, buckboards, pack mules and horses, but not stagecoaches.

Charity and Mitchell were first out of the coach

and Mitchell took his hand as he walked into the inn with Charity. A man in rimless spectacles and with thinning hair looked up from behind a desk. "I wrote ahead for reservations," Charity said. "Mitchell Blake and Charity Foster."

"Yes, ma'am, we have your letter. You're in rooms three and four," the clerk said and glanced at Fargo. "You'll be wanting a room, too?" he asked.

"I think I've got a room," Fargo said and the desk clerk looked perplexed as Charity turned away with a smug little smile. "I could stand a drink," Fargo said and the clerk motioned to a large room that seemed to combine a dining room and lobby. Fargo glanced at Charity and she nodded.

"I'd like that," she said. He started toward the room when Pauline came up, her bag in hand.

"How about a drink with us?" Fargo asked and the snapping blue eyes crackled.

"I'm buying," she said. "As many as you like. It'll be my pleasure. Go on in. I'll be along in a minute."

Fargo stepped into the room where half of the space was taken by round tables, the other half lounging chairs. Charity lowered herself wearily into a chair at the nearest table and Mitchell quickly sat between her and Fargo. "When do we go to grandpa's?" he asked Charity.

"Tomorrow," she said. "I imagine someone will be sent looking for us."

"You've got to come, Fargo," Mitchell said and Fargo nodded agreement as Pauline came in and sat down. An elderly man shuffled to the table with a cork-lined tray.

"Bourbon," Fargo ordered and Pauline and Charity had the same.

"Lemonade," Mitchell said in his most grown-up voice and the old man shuffled away. Fargo glimpsed Myrna and Ferris as they went to the desk to register.

"Tomorrow's the fifteenth," Fargo said to Charity. "No bonus days."

"I'm just glad we're here," Charity said and he felt her hand touch his thigh under the table.

"That makes two of us," Pauline said. "I didn't think you could keep pulling us through, Fargo. But you did."

The voice cut into the conversation, deep and smooth. "Mitchell," it called. "We've been waiting for you." Fargo looked up and saw the man approaching, tall, well-dressed in a gray frock coat and blue cravat, a darkly handsome face with black hair and a small black mustache. He heard Charity's gasp of surprise beside him as the man halted at the table. "Hello, Charity," he said with a smoothly controlled smile.

"Hello," Charity said and almost gasped out the word.

"We thought we'd surprise you," the man said.

"You certainly have. We? Is Mrs. Blake here?" Charity asked.

"She is indeed," the man said.

"My mom's here?" Mitchell exploded. "Wow. Where is she?"

"At your grandpa's," the man said and brought his eyes to Fargo. "I'm Joe Tacks. I'm a friend of Paula Blake."

"He's Ma's boyfriend," Mitchell cut in.

"I'm sorry, I didn't mean to be rude. I was just so surprised," Charity said. "Joe Tacks, this is Skye Fargo. We wouldn't be here if it weren't for him."

"Really?" the man said. "You've got to tell me all about it at the house."

"How come you and Mom are here?" Mitchell asked.

"Your mother decided to make it a family reunion, a last-minute decision. We had to ride long and hard to get here," Joe Tacks said.

"I sure want to see Mom and Grandpa," Mitchell said.

"Sure thing, Mitchell," the man said and turned to Charity. "I've a buckboard and a driver outside. He'll take you and Mitchell to his grandpa's place. I know Paula will have all kinds of questions about the trip."

"We'll have all kinds of things to tell her," Charity said.

"Will we ever," Mitchell chimed in.

"I'll be along later," the man said and swept everyone with another smooth smile. He paused at Fargo and gave the smile an extra emphasis. "I'm sure we'll be talking again," he said. "Thanks for taking such good care of Mitchell and Charity." He tossed a quick smile at Mitchell and strode away and Fargo felt Mitchell tug at his arm.

"You come with us, Fargo," the boy said.

"Maybe tomorrow," Fargo said and rested a hand on the tousled head. "I'm sure your ma would rather see you alone first."

"I don't know why she didn't come along with Joe Tacks," Charity remarked.

"You know Ma," Mitchell answered. "She'd rather sit and wait."

"Wait for me outside, Mitchell," Charity said. "I'll be right along. Get our bags from the stage." Mitchell nodded and raced away, excitement in his every movement. Charity handed Fargo her key. "I'll be back, as quickly as I can," she said. "I'll have Joe Tacks drive me back if I have to."

Fargo smiled at her as he took the key. "You surprise me. In front of Pauline? What happened to all the properness?" he asked.

"I guess I'm getting as contradictory as you." She laughed and hurried away. Fargo sat down as the man returned with the drinks and Pauline lifted her glass in a salute.

"To you, young feller," she said and took a deep draw of her bourbon that spoke of years of experience. "You staying around for a spell?" she asked.

"Depends," he said.

"On Charity?" she slid at him and he grinned. "I'd say you'll be around for a good spell, then," the little old lady chortled. "I'll be getting a rig tomorrow. My brother's place is some twenty miles west. You'll be welcome there anytime, Fargo."

"Thanks," Fargo said. "I might just drop by."

"Mitchell's ma must be a strange woman," Pauline mused aloud. "She sends the boy all the way out on a stage with his governess and then decides to rush out and meet him here with her boyfriend."

"Guilty conscience, maybe," Fargo said. "I got the feeling she's more interested in boyfriends than

in being a mother. That's why she hired Charity."
He paused as Ferris and Myrna came into the room
and sat down at a table in the far corner, drew his
eyes from them and took a deep sip of his bourbon.

"Some answers stay out of reach," Pauline said
and there was understanding in her voice. "You'll
never stop wondering. I probably won't, either."

"Got any candidates?" Fargo asked grimly.

"Marge, I'm afraid. A jilted lover can go crazy.
Many have killed before," Pauline said. "But maybe
that's just the woman in me talking. You figure it's
Ferris?"

"Holman," Fargo said. "Zeb Jonah said the man
pulling the strings was called Tex. I can't stop thinking that could be one of the cattlemen Holman
ruined."

"Damn near everybody who's ever been in Texas
is called that," Pauline said. "And maybe he heard
wrong."

Fargo grimaced. "He said he heard it twice. Tex.
Tex," Fargo muttered as he stared into his bourbon
and suddenly he felt the coldness sweep through
him, as though an icy hand had reached inside him
to freeze his blood.

"What is it?" Pauline asked as she saw his fingers curl around the glass so tightly they turned
white.

"Maybe he didn't hear wrong," Fargo said. "Only
it wasn't Tex. Maybe it was Tacks." He stared into
Pauline's eyes as she stared back.

"Tacks, like in Joe Tacks," she breathed.

"Goddamn," Fargo rasped as he stood up. "That's
it. Jonah heard the name Tacks and took it as Tex.

Goddamn!" He stared at Pauline as he heard his own words whirl inside him with a wild, bitter laughter, mocking as they chilled. "They were after Mitchell," he muttered. "Goddamn, they were after Mitchell."

The table almost upended as he hit against it, raced from the room and glimpsed Ferris and Myrna look up in surprise. It was near dark outside as he skidded to a halt and scanned the ground in front of the inn. The wheel marks were clear and he saw the buckboard had pulled sharply away from the hitching post. Fargo vaulted onto the Ovaro and swung behind the tracks of the buckboard and he saw the rig had put on speed the moment it left town, the prints of the horse digging hard into the ground. He leaned low in the saddle as the light grew faint and saw where the buckboard had left the road to climb a low hill. The tracks of two horses came in to flank the wagon as it climbed the hill to the top. Fargo slowed as he crested the hill and saw that the buckboard had gone down the other side to where a narrow road led north.

He swore as the last of the daylight faded away and he reined up, slid from the horse and began to follow the trail on foot. The moon hadn't climbed high enough yet to afford help but he felt his way with his feet, using touch to follow the tracks of the buckboard. It was painfully slow as he slid along the ground in the wheel marks and he was grateful to see the moon rise. With enough pale light to pick up tracks he swung onto the Ovaro and went on. The buckboard climbed a sudden steep turn in the road and Fargo followed to find the road leveled off at the top. He reined up as he caught the pinpoint of yellow light some hundred yards on. Keeping the pinto at a walk, he moved closer and a small house took shape, the light coming from two windows. He saw the buckboard outside and six horses at a long hitching post.

Fargo swung to the ground and crept forward, saw both windows were open and the voices from inside sounded clearly as he dropped to a crouch and crept to the house. He heard Charity, her words clipped out with precision, as though she were lecturing a recalcitrant child. "You can't do this. Grandfather Blake will hear that the stage arrived," she said.

"And he'll hear about the accident that happened to you and the kid," Joe Tacks said with smooth confidence. "That road we took goes past a sharp drop-off only a dozen yards from here. You were driving too fast and went over. A real tragedy."

"My ma wouldn't let you do this," Fargo heard Mitchell blurt out. "You've got her tied up, too, someplace. I know it."

Joe Tacks laughed, a harsh sound. "Yeah, I've got her tied up, but differently," he said.

"You piece of slime," Charity flung at him and Fargo heard the sharp sound of a slap.

"Nobody talks to Joe Tacks that way," the man snarled. "I'm going to let my boys enjoy you tonight, sort of a bonus for them, not that they earned it. They should've finished off the whole damn stagecoach the first time around."

"You couldn't ever beat Fargo," Mitchell shouted. "Not ever ever."

"Shut up," Tacks snapped. Fargo moved closer to the open windows. He'd heard no reasons, no explanation for any of it but that was unimportant now. He halted where he could peer over the window ledge and into the room. Mitchell and Charity were seated in straight-backed chairs, side by side, with Joe Tacks in front of them. The five hired guns lounged against the walls of the room. They were too far apart to bring down with one volley, Fargo saw. He'd have to even the odds, first. Staying low, he crept to the hinged side of the door, unholstered the big Colt and held it by the barrel.

He made a thumping sound against the side of the house, an undefined sound that could have been made by almost anything. "What was that?" he heard Tacks bark instantly.

"'A raccoon, maybe," one of the hired guns said.

"Don't give me maybes. Go see, dammit," Tacks snapped.

Fargo raised the Colt as the door opened and the man stepped out into the night. He let the door swing shut behind him as he blinked, adjusted his eyes to the dark. Fargo brought the butt of the gun down hard on the top of the man's head and caught him with his other hand as he started to collapse. He laid him gently against the house and returned to the door. Only a few moments passed when he heard Joe Tacks call out. "Edwards?" the man shouted and only silence answered. Tacks's voice carried more irritation than concern. "Two of you go see what the hell he's doing out there," he ordered and Fargo swore under his breath. He couldn't put two away silently. He'd have to move boldly. But the odds would be cut in half when he finished.

The two figures stepped out of the door, peered into the night. Fargo had the Colt in position to fire but he didn't like shooting down even hired guns in cold blood. He'd give them a chance though he knew damn well what would happen. "Drop your guns," he said quietly. "Nice and slow." The two men whirled, both drawing at once and Fargo sighed as two shots exploded from the Colt. Both men staggered back, seemed to do a strange little dance together as they twisted and collapsed in unison.

"Shit." Fargo heard the shout from inside the house and he threw himself prone on the ground. The two remaining gunslingers barreled out of the doorway, spraying an arc of bullets both left and right. Fargo fired from on his stomach as the bullets whistled through the air over his head. His first shot tore into the nearest man's abdomen and the figure doubled over as though jackknifed. His second shot caught the other man at an angle, the heavy shell passing through his ribs and out of his chest. Twin streams of red gushed out of him as he fell. Fargo rolled, came up against the side of the house, taking the moment to reload.

"Come out, Tacks. Hands in the air," he called but it was Charity's voice that answered.

"He took Mitchell. He went out the back window," she said and he saw her appear in the doorway.

"Stay here." Fargo whirled and started around the back of the house, then slowed at the corner as he saw the figure with the small form clutched in front of him. Joe Tacks held his gun to Mitchell's temple.

"Back off or the kid gets his head blown away," the man said and Fargo stayed, his mouth a thin line. Tacks moved forward, Mitchell held securely in front of him. "Back off, I said," he repeated and Fargo heard him draw the hammer back on the gun. He moved slowly backward as his finger on the trigger of the Colt itched to fire the gun. But Mitchell was a dead boy, even if his shot managed to hit Tacks. The man's gun would go off, his finger tightening on the trigger in an automatic reflex. Tacks moved toward the horses and Fargo circled along a line of shrubs. "Don't move," Tacks snarled.

"Go to hell," Fargo said and stepped closer to the shrubs.

"Stay there, you son-of-a-bitch," the man shouted.

"Shoot me," Fargo said and saw Tacks almost pull the gun from Mitchell's temple. But he stopped himself and kept the gunbarrel against the boy.

"Good try, you big bastard," Tacks snarled as he reached the horses. He stopped at a big gray and Fargo saw that the gun at Mitchell's temple never wavered. "Throw that Colt away," the man ordered.

"Let the boy go, first," Fargo said.

"You think I'm a goddamn fool?" Tacks said. "Throw the gun away or the kid gets it."

"You kill him and you're a dead man," Fargo said. "Guaranteed."

"Maybe, but the kid's dead first," the man countered and Fargo swore silently. Joe Tacks had lost. He had only his life left and desperation made a man's mind work in strange ways. Mitchell was

170

his last bargaining chip. He wouldn't throw it away lightly. But he could act out of rage and frustration. Reasons didn't much matter. What mattered was Mitchell's young life. Fargo slowly unclasped his hand and let the Colt drop to the ground. "Kick it over here," the man ordered. "All the way over here."

Fargo drew his foot back and kicked the Colt, swore as he watched it skitter across the ground almost to the man's feet. He tightened calf and thigh muscles, grimly certain of what the man would do. But he had a half-second, the time it would take for Tacks to bring the gun down from Mitchell's temple and take aim. He flung himself over in a backflip, crashed into the high shrubs and rolled as two shots exploded and he heard the bullets smash into the ground where he'd been. He rolled again, heard the man curse and lifted his head to see Joe Tacks scoop up the Colt, throw Mitchell facedown across the gray and leap into the saddle.

"No, no," Charity screamed as she ran across the ground but Joe Tacks was disappearing into the trees. Fargo passed her with long legs flying as he raced for the Ovaro and vaulted onto the horse. He could still hear the man's horse crashing through brush and he sent the pinto into a gallop. The tree cover thinned and he saw Tacks turn to look back at him. He flattened himself across the pinto's withers as two shots flew past, fired with too much haste and far wide of their target. He kept the pinto charging forward, directly behind the racing gray and he saw Tacks turn and fire another two shots. These were closer, Fargo noted as he stayed flattened against the horse. Tacks had emptied his gun with the six shots but he also had the Colt and Fargo turned to see him fire again. This time one shot nicked the corner of the saddle horn as the pinto closed within yards of the other horse. Fargo let out a groan and dropped from the horse, braced himself and landed on his shoulder and rolled to lay still.

He heard Joe Tacks rein up. The man was a determined, ruthless killer. He'd come back to enjoy victory or finish the job if need be. Fargo's hand stole down along his leg to the calf holster where the double-edged throwing knife rested. He heard the slow sound of the horse being walked back and drew the knife out. Joe Tacks came into sight, the Colt still in his hand but held casually. "It looks like I'm still going to win, boy," he heard the man say to the small figure draped across the saddle.

Fargo flung the razor-sharp, thin blade with a powerful flick of his wrist, let his forearm follow through. He saw Tacks's eyes grow wide in surprise and he tried to raise the Colt. But the throwing knife hurtled through the air and slammed into the base of his throat. Joe Tacks quivered, dropped the Colt and brought both hands up to where the knife was embedded in him. He yanked it free and a gusher of red followed as he half-fell, half-dropped from the horse. He stayed on his hands and knees for a moment as blood flowed from him as though he were a fountain. Somehow, out of fury and hate, he rose up, tried to reach for the Colt. Fargo let a left hook crash into the side of his head. "That's for

Mitchell," he said as the man toppled. Joe Tacks fell into a growing red pool, coughed and was still.

Fargo glanced up and saw Mitchell slide from the gray and rush to him. He held the boy tightly until the small form stopped trembling. "Time to get back to Charity," he said and put Mitchell on the Ovaro and swung in beside him. He rode back at a fast canter and saw Charity standing where he'd left her in front of the house. She exploded in a cry of relief as he rode up and Mitchell slid from the horse into her arms. "You and Mitchell take the buckboard," Fargo said. "You want to fill me in?"

"Mitchell's grandpa is going to make Mitchell the heir to his considerable fortune," Charity said as she started to drive. "That's why he wanted Mitchell here by the fifteenth. That is the deadline for transferring certain deeds and documents and Mitchell's signature was needed."

"You didn't know anything about this?" Fargo put in.

"No, nothing," Charity said. "Tacks was talkative. He was bragging, in fact. He'd smooth-talked Paula Blake into agreeing to marry him. If something happened to Mitchell, she'd inherit everything."

"So he decided to make that all come about," Fargo said. "A Crow attack wiping out the whole stage would've been perfect."

"Only you stopped that, Fargo," Mitchell said.

"We'll get you to your grandpa in the morning. We could all use a good night's sleep tonight," Fargo said.

"Or something," Charity muttered and hurried

the buckboard on. He rode beside her and they finally reached town and the inn. Holman, Ferris and Marge O'Day were waiting in the lobby when he entered with Mitchell and Charity and he saw Pauline to one side. She shook her head admiringly and blew him a kiss.

"Pauline told us," Ferris said. "Of course, we figured something was wrong when you ran out of here. It seems you owe us an apology."

Fargo frowned at the man, let his eyes take in Marge and Holman. He slowly drew the Colt from its holster. "One of you swindled his company and cheated his accomplice; one of you sold rotten medicine and ruined four cattlemen and one of you ran out on a lover and stole his money. You all lied to me. You want an apology?" Fargo said. "I'll give you one. You've got three minutes to clear out of here before I tell you how sorry I am that I'm taking you all back to pay up for your crimes." His eyes were blue stone as he saw Ferris swallow, glance at the others. Almost in unison, they turned and rushed from the room.

Pauline came forward, her face crinkled with a broad grin. "You'd do it and they know it," she said.

"I have other plans but they don't need to know that," Fargo said as he led Charity away. He waited while she saw Mitchell into his room and in bed and he was undressed in the dark when she returned to her adjoining room.

"I was beginning to think I'd never get another chance," Charity said and he heard her pull off clothes. She came to him, warm, softly curving breasts pressed into his chest. She kissed him hungrily, let her tongue play with his, then brought one modest breast up for his lips, shivered as he drew it in and closed his teeth gently against the tiny pink tip. She made love with a new abandon, every part of her giving, no doubts any longer and when she flowed around him and screamed in that final moment of absolute pleasure she fell back and clung to him until she lay satiated, drawing in deep breaths.

Later, she rose onto her side and her hand explored his body, caressed and enjoyed every part of him, a combination of discovery and delight. "Maybe you're not really a contradiction at all," Fargo commented. "Maybe you're just all sinner."

"Or all saint." She laughed and they made love again and the night finally wore to a close as he slept with her slender warmth against him. He rose when morning came and felt a different kind of sourness in his mouth and she was quick to catch his mood. "What is it?" she asked.

"Tell you after you take Mitchell to his grandpa," Fargo said and saw her to the buckboard. Mitchell clung to him for a long moment.

"Promise you'll come visit grandpa and me," Mitchell said.

"Promise," Fargo answered and the boy finally released his hold on him. Charity stopped to get directions from the general store and he watched the buckboard disappear down the road. He returned to the room, undressed and relaxed; it was late afternoon when Charity returned. She sank wearily but contentedly onto the bed next to him.

"Everything went well. He's a fine old man," she said, "and he's waiting for a visit from you. Mitchell told him everything that had happened, of course. I hardly had anything to add." She paused, studied him for a moment. "You want to tell me what's still bothering you?" she said.

"I keep wondering how much Mitchell's mother knew about all of it," he said. "Seems she's pretty much out for herself."

"Tacks said it was his idea," Charity said.

"That doesn't say she didn't know about it."

"No, it doesn't."

"Hate to think about the boy going back to her if she did know. She might find another boyfriend and another scheme," Fargo said.

"It doesn't matter," Charity said.

"What do you mean it doesn't matter?" Fargo snapped and sat up. "Talk about contradictions. What the hell kind of a remark is that?"

Charity smiled at him. "Mitchell really got to you, didn't he?" she said.

"He's a good kid. He doesn't deserve a damn tarantula for a mother," Fargo said. "He doesn't deserve a damn governess who thinks it doesn't matter, either."

He frowned at the smile that persisted on her lips. "It doesn't matter because his grandfather's started custody proceedings for him and he's hired me to stay on," Charity said with a trace of smugness. She turned, came against him. "Does he deserve a governess who's becoming a sex fiend?" she asked.

"Definitely," Fargo said. "A governess is supposed to know everything about everything."

"I need more lessons. Will you stay on?" she asked.

"For a while," Fargo said. "We'll have speed practice right now."

"Speed practice?" Charity frowned.

"Yes, let's see how fast you can get that damn dress off," he said and lay back as Charity flew into action. He'd stay on some, he thought and smiled. Hell, if a pumpkin could turn into a fancy carriage, a stagecoach to hell could turn into a pleasure trip.

LOOKING FORWARD!

**The following is the opening
section from the next novel in the exciting
Trailsman series from Signet:**

THE TRAILSMAN #59
FARGO'S WOMAN

*Southwestern Minnesota, 1861—
an unfriendly land, where good comfort
and a good woman were equally hard to find. . . .*

The Trailsman was weary, not with the simple
fatigue that comes from physical effort but with
the soul-deep weariness of discouragement. He was
disheartened. He'd had a lead to the men he sought
that had taken him over a long trail and a hard
ride. Now he had nothing, nothing at all. It was as
if the men who had gunned down his family never
existed.

They had been said to be here. His informant had
been sure of it. But no one here had ever heard of
them. No one confessed to ever having seen them.
It was as if they had dropped off the edges of the
earth. Skye Fargo's spur rowels were dragging as he
glanced toward the livery at the edge of the town.

But that was several hundred yards away, and the black and white stallion was well bedded, taken into the care of a man who seemed to know what he was doing. The hell with it. Just this once, the hell with it. Let the old hostler do his job. Fargo pushed through the strings of fly-beads that curtained the door of the nearest saloon. He wanted a drink to numb the storm of memory that had been flooding his thoughts ever since he heard his quarry was said to be within reach.

"Whiskey," he ordered in a dull, flat voice.

The bartender complied and accepted Fargo's money. Fargo left his change where it was, tossed off the first fiery drink and ordered another. He shuddered, the bite of the trade whiskey eating at his throat like acid, the heat of it spreading into his gut.

Fargo stood at the bar paying scant attention to the others in the place, although years of gun-caution had become habit; he remained more alert now than most men would at their best.

He was an imposing figure there, his lean height apparent even as he bent to the bar, his hair curling a gleaming black where it spilled, long uncut, from beneath the crown of his hat, his lake-blue eyes in constant motion as he assessed his surroundings as naturally and automatically as he breathed.

"Another?"

"Sure," the Trailsman answered. The bartender poured from a grimy, often-refilled bottle and sorted the payment from the loose change on the bar.

"You look like you've come a far piece," the barman observed.

"Farther'n you'll ever know."

The bartender nodded sympathetically and topped off Fargo's glass again, this time on the house. The man glanced toward the other end of the long bar and raised his chin in a slight, almost unnoticeable gesture. Within moments there was a girl at Fargo's side. She had been idling down at the end of the bar with a glass in front of her. The glass held an amber liquid that could have been whiskey but that almost certainly was not.

Fargo's suspicion was confirmed when he faced her. She was exceptionally tall and not unattractive, her rouged and powdered face coming within inches of Fargo's. Her breath was clean, with no hint of liquor on it. But she smelled nice, of soap more than of perfume. She was wearing a high-waisted dress that emphasized her breasts beneath the covering of scarlet cloth but which was otherwise oddly decorous. The dress covered her from throat to shoe-tips, and its sleeves extended down to her gloved hands. It was damned odd for a saloon girl's costume.

Then, laughing happily, she turned to show him the back of the outfit. There was no back to it. Except for a few thin strings to hold things together, the modest dress was a false front. Her backside was completely exposed. And she was wearing no underthings.

Fargo smiled and saluted her with his glass. She had a damned fine figure.

"I'm Wilma," she said. "And you are . . . ?"

"Skye," he told her. He paused for a moment, wide-eyed and unblinking. For just a moment, without conscious thought, he had very nearly blurted out the name he had not used in all the time since his family died. There was something about this Wilma, something in the clarity of her gray eyes, perhaps something in the curve of her lips, that touched him. It was something he could not put a name to. But something he could feel.

Fargo motioned for the bartender to set Wilma up to a glass of tepid tea. While the man was pouring from the special bottle, Fargo looked into those large, gray eyes. He expected Wilma to be paying attention to her employer. Instead she was looking back into the cool blue of Fargo's stare.

Her lips twitched, as if she had been about to give him a professional smile, but that expression was stillborn. Instead she looked at him seriously. As if she was seeing far beyond the surface the Trailsman presented to the world at large. Her breath caught in her throat for an instant. Then she reached out with a slender hand to touch his wrist. No more than that. Just a simple touch on the wrist. But it felt to Fargo as if she had burnt him with an iron.

"Fargo," he said in response to her unspoken question. It was eerie, but he knew what she was about to ask. He knew her question as easily as if she had already asked it.

She smiled and moved closer to him without pawing or even touching him. She was close enough that he could sense the warmth from her slim body. He felt more aroused by this woman's nearness than he would have been by a blatant fondling from any other saloon girl he had ever known. There was something about her. . . .

Wilma looked at him and smiled. There was nothing artificial about it. No fluttering of her eyelashes. No manufactured coyness. She smiled at him and she sighed, and there was a quick sparking of deep happiness in her eyes now when she looked at him. Fargo felt the weariness slip away from him. This was a woman a man could draw comfort from.

"I'm hungry," Fargo said. Minutes before he had been too tired for hunger. Now, suddenly, he was not.

"We have all the time in the world," Wilma said gently.

"I know," Fargo responded, smiling now for the first time in days.

"You do know, don't you?" Wilma said. "You feel it too."

"Yes." Fargo smiled again. He bent his head and kissed her. The contact was light and unhurried. Her lips molded softly to his. Her mouth had a fresh, clean flavor, as if she was untouched by whatever it was that had brought her here.

She was a saloon whore in a half-assed little

Excerpt from FARGO'S WOMAN

Minnesota town. And neither Skye Fargo nor she cared about that a whit. When she gave herself to him it would be pure and fresh in all the ways that mattered.

"Join me?" he offered.

Wilma shook her head. Fargo noticed that before he had thought her not unattractive. Now he found her to be beautiful. "I can't leave."

"I'll be back."

She smiled. "I know."

He kissed her again and went to find a restaurant. He no longer felt tired at all. Instead he felt . . . it had been so very long that he had difficulty identifying the sensation for a moment . . . content.

Damn. Contentment? How very strange. But how very nice, the Trailsman thought.

He felt good when he pushed through the fly beads and re-entered the little saloon. His supper lay warm and satisfying in his belly, and for the first time in many years he felt almost at peace. He was in no hurry.

The saloon was busier than it had been when he left. It was evening, and the drinking trade had picked up as freighters and farmers and businessmen put the day's work aside.

Most of the patrons were drinking slowly and talking in low tones. One rough-looking group in the corner was loud. No one seemed to mind. Certainly Skye Fargo did not.

Wilma was not in the place. Fargo felt no alarm,

not even—and it surprised him to realize it—disappointment. She would be back. He was sure of that. He ordered a drink, a beer this time, as a time-killer, and leaned against the bar.

"Got a message for you," the bartender said as he delivered the foamy beer.

"I know," Fargo said with a smile. "Wilma said she won't be long."

The barman blinked. "How'd you know that?"

Fargo shrugged, and the bartender let it pass. He had other customers to tend to.

A back door opened, letting a breeze flow through the saloon to eddy the smoke of a good many pipes and cigars, and Wilma came inside, followed closely by a large man in coveralls and a flannel shirt. The man was hatless and sweaty. He had one big hand cupped over the right cheek of Wilma's exposed rump.

Fargo took no offense. He knew what Wilma was, how she earned her living. That had nothing to do with the qualities that lay under the surface.

Fargo pondered that for a moment and was pleased, and a trifle surprised, to realize that it genuinely made no difference. This stranger's business dealings had nothing to do with what Wilma offered to Skye Fargo.

She saw Fargo and smiled, turned her head and said something to the big man.

The fellow scowled and motioned toward the table full of loud-talking, heavy-drinking men in the far corner. Wilma smiled and shook her head in apology. She tried to cross the room toward Fargo.

"No!" the big man bellowed. He grabbed her roughly by the arm and tried to force her toward the table.

Fargo straightened. He started forward.

"Our money's good here, bitch." The big man glared at the bartender and said, "This hoor needs a strappin', bud, and I'm just the man to give it to her."

The son-of-a-bitch cuffed Wilma, backhanding her and sending her reeling against the bar with blood streaming from her nose and mouth.

The bartender grabbed up a hickory ax handle, but Fargo was there before him. Fargo's right fist flashed out, catching the man flush on the mouth, crushing flesh between fist and teeth and splitting the man's lips. Fargo whipped a low, hard left into the man's gut and followed it with a right to the throat that dropped the fellow to the floor, gagging and puking.

He could hear boot heels on the puncheon floor behind him as one of the big man's friends jumped in. He whirled and met the charge, ducked under a wild right and pummeled the newcomer with a vicious series of lefts and rights.

Neither the big man nor his friends appeared to be armed. Fargo ignored the Colt belted at his waist, set his feet wide and concentrated on cutting the man down with quick, calculated blows.

A fist glancing off the back of his skull was the

first indication that these sons-of-bitches liked to fight in bunches.

The big man who had started it all was on his feet again, grappling with the bartender, while two or maybe three of them concentrated on Skye Fargo.

Fargo spun as one of them tried to pin his arms from behind. His elbow smashed into the man's face, and Fargo could hear the pop as bone shattered. The man screamed and went pale except for the bright red of the blood that was spurting from his nostrils. A kick coming seemingly from nowhere missed its mark and thudded into Fargo's thigh.

All right, dammit, their rules, Fargo thought.

He whirled back to his right. That man with the broken face was still back there and still on his feet. Fargo thumped a backhanded fist onto the bastard's broken jaw, then spun to his left and launched a kick of his own aimed for the kicker's balls.

Fargo's left leg, numbed by the impact of that first unexpected kick, weakened, and he lurched sideways, almost losing his balance and his boot landed off target. Something hard slammed into the small of Fargo's back, driving him forward, and one of the attackers swung a wild, looping overhand punch that smashed into Fargo's left eye, nearly closing it.

Fargo blinked the blood away in time to see another punch coming in. He flicked it aside with his forearm and delivered a straight right that jarred him all the way up to the shoulder. How it must have felt at the other end was satisfying to imagine.

Wilma was in the fray too, Fargo noticed. She was riding high on the big man's back, raking at his eyes with her fingernails and with her teeth clamped in his ear. The big bastard spun and gouged, having no success in ridding himself of Wilma but managing to knock the bartender on his ass with his blindly frantic swings and punches.

A body came flying in from Fargo's near-blind left side, sending Fargo and at least two other men to the floor. They were grappling, pummeling, throwing fists and knees and elbows. Fargo returned the effort, squirming and lashing out at whatever was near enough to reach. Someone fell on top of him. The man had eaten something with garlic in it recently. There was a salty, copper taste of blood in Fargo's mouth.

He punched hard and fast, rolled, twisted, came to his knees. He chopped down with the edge of his left hand, slashing it across the bridge of one man's nose. Fargo drove an elbow into another one's gut and immediately regretted that as a sour spray of vomit spewed over his back and shoulders.

There seemed to be three of them plus the big guy who had started it all. Fargo banged one in the jaw, came weaving onto his feet and kicked someone square in the cods.

The odds were beginning to come down to close to even.

Fargo ducked under the flash of a swung bottle

and crunched a hard right into the man's chest. The blow landed over the man's heart and stopped him in his tracks. Arm weary and gasping for breath, Fargo surveyed the bloody scene with his one good eye and turned to face the big son-of-a-bitch who was still trying to pry Wilma off his back.

Fargo limped forward, favoring his left leg, and punched the son-of-a-bitch in the mouth hard enough to break three teeth. And hard enough to damn near break Skye Fargo's hand in the process. The big man shuddered and went down, spilling himself and the spitting fury that was Wilma onto the floor.

Fargo was close to exhaustion. But the others had to be just as bad off or worse. He reeled backward, bumping into somebody, blinking away the flow of blood that continued to flood his left eye. Something slammed into Fargo's back, low and hard.

He turned, but slowly. His legs were not working the way they should and his knees were giving out on him.

That shouldn't be.

His vision grew misty. Everything in front of him looked like it was under pink-colored and cloudy water.

The man who had been behind him was the one with the broken jaw. The fellow had a knife in his hand stained bright red with Skye Fargo's blood.

Fargo groped for the butt of his Colt.

He heard Wilma scream, but distantly. It was as

if she was far away and standing in the bottom of a well. Her voice sounded hollow to him.

Fargo fell forward, grabbing for the bar to help support him. His knees wouldn't do that job any longer. He had the Colt in his hand, but he could no longer remember what he wanted it for.

Then the mist closed over him, and he had a sudden sensation of floating.

Then he was aware of nothing.

Of nothing at all.